"You know, I'm worried about you, Morea."

Ridge continued, "Probably the next thing you'll forget is that this scheme of your mother's, this engagement, is only make-believe, and—"

"Don't lose any sleep over that possibility."

Ridge didn't seem to hear. "Then you'll start acting as if we're really serious about each other—"

"Not a chance, Coltrain."

"And I'll no doubt end up having to marry you after all!"

Morea was speechless....

In **The Perfect Divorce!** (#3444), Synnamon Welles needed help saving her marriage. She turned to her best friend, Morea—and now Morea finds her own unexpected romance in this terrific follow-up story:

The Fake Fiancé!

Leigh Michaels has always loved happy endings. Even when she was a child, if a book's conclusion didn't please her, she'd make up her own. And though she always wanted to write fiction, she very sensibly planned to earn her living as a newspaper reporter. That career didn't work out, however, and she found herself writing for Harlequin instead—in the kind of happy ending only a romance novelist could dream up!

Leigh loves to hear from readers; you can write to her at P.O. Box 935, Ottumwa, Iowa, 52501-0935 U.S.A.

Books by Leigh Michaels

The Fake Fiancé!
Leigh Michaels

Harlequin Books

TORONTO • NEW YORK • LONDON
AMSTERDAM • PARIS • SYDNEY • HAMBURG
STOCKHOLM • ATHENS • TOKYO • MILAN
MADRID • WARSAW • BUDAPEST • AUCKLAND

IN MEMORY OF
Bill Dew
friend and attorney
who helped to plot this story

ISBN 0-373-03478-4

THE FAKE FIANCÉ!

First North American Publication 1997.

CHAPTER ONE

THE perpetual shadow of the parking garage kept the air cooler inside than it was outdoors, but the same stillness which banished Denver's summer heat held exhaust fumes prisoner within the concrete structure. Morea Landon wrinkled her nose in distaste as she opened the door of her silver BMW and felt stale air hit her full in the face. She took a deep breath anyway and started across the ramp toward the skywalk entrance to the office building.

Her private parking spot was the farthest away from the building in the long row reserved for the partners in her law practice. In a firm like Taylor Bradley Cummings, seniority counted not only in office assignments and executive dining room privileges but in parking—and Morea, though she'd been at TBC for almost three years, had been a junior partner for only six months.

It's good for you to walk farther, she told herself. At least this way, on days when she was too busy to go to the gym, she got a little exercise.

She cut across an almost-empty row of parking spaces much nearer the entrance. *Reserved for clients of Taylor Bradley Cummings*, a large sign above each spot warned. Only one of the spots, the one closest to the door, was occupied; the lunch hour wasn't quite over yet, and if any of TBC's exclusive, upscale clients needed legal advice at the moment, they were probably ensconced with their attorneys over martinis in the dining room of a private club.

She frowned as she walked around the single car, a battered-looking convertible with multicolored fenders. It hardly looked like the sort of thing TBC's clients drove. The car wasn't old enough to be antique, or stylish enough to be classic. And as a matter of fact, Morea thought, it could probably account, all by itself, for the aroma of exhaust fumes in the garage.

Then she saw the personalized license plate. *Ridge*, it said crisply—as if anyone who saw it didn't need to know more.

Morea sighed. There was no point in being petty; there was plenty of space. And she supposed that technically Ridge Coltrain was eligible to park in TBC's reserved area this afternoon. While he wasn't a client, he did have an appointment on the penthouse floor— with Morea herself, to discuss the breakup of the Madisons' marriage. Again.

He was early, too. Morea glanced at her watch and wondered why he'd appeared so far ahead of schedule. He might, of course, be up in the waiting room with the Madison file spread out on a coffee table, doing a little last minute practicing of what he was going to say to her...

Not likely, she decided. *Ridge Coltrain's so sure of himself he'd walk on stage to do* Hamlet *without bothering to rehearse.*

The really annoying thing was that he could probably pull it off.

She still had fifteen minutes before her appointment, and she wasn't about to show up a moment early. *Never let an opponent think you might be nervous*, one of her law school professors had said, and anticipating meeting times was one of the giveaways.

Morea only wished she dared believe that the rule applied in reverse. If Ridge was feeling jittery about the

Madisons' property settlement...but in her experience, Ridge Coltrain never felt anxious about anything.

At any rate, she had plenty of time to pick up her messages, answer any questions her secretary might have about work in progress, straighten her hair and reapply her lipstick...

Not, of course, that she was trying to impress Ridge. It was simply good strategy to always look her best in any professional encounter, whether in her own office, an opponent's, or in court.

Besides, nothing but a good legal argument made any impression on the man. He was absolutely impervious to appearances and niceties, so things like sidelong looks and batted eyelashes would probably go straight over his head.

Not that she had any desire to practice feminine wiles on him, anyway, Morea assured herself. Any such attempt would not only be useless, it'd be unprofessional.

She pulled open the skywalk door just as a woman came out of the building. Morea stopped dead in her tracks. "Mother? What are you doing here?"

Meredith Landon was almost as tall as her daughter, and in her youth her hair had been the same silky midnight black as Morea's. Now she was almost sixty, her hair was naturally silver, and she wore it cut extremely short to emphasize the strong, beautiful bones in her face. "Hello, Morea. I just came downtown to run an errand."

"Darn—I wish I'd known. We haven't had a chance to really talk for a couple of weeks. We could have gone out for lunch together."

"Well, I didn't have any idea when I'd be finished— so don't feel badly at missing me, dear."

"But I do," Morea protested. "I only went out for lunch to get a little fresh air and perspective before I

have to spend the afternoon in conference. I'd much
rather have a chance to talk to you."

"That's flattering, dear. Don't let me keep you away
from your work, though."

"I've got a few minutes. My appointment isn't till
half-past one. So tell me about your errand, Mom. Is that
a brand-new haircut? It looks a bit different somehow."

"My watch says it's twenty-seven past, Morea."

Stunned, Morea stared at the digital display on
Meredith's watch, and then in disbelief consulted the
tiny jeweled bauble on her own wrist. The hands hadn't
moved since the last time she'd glanced at it. "Oh,
damn," she said under her breath. "Wouldn't you know
it, the battery would pick today to die just because it's
Ridge Coltrain waiting for me. If I'm half a minute late,
he'll never let me forget it. The man's a jinx... I'll call
you later, Mom."

She hurried down the corridor and around the corner
to the elevator lobby, hoping that the express to the penthouse floor would be waiting. The inside of the elevator
door was polished stainless steel, and though it was a
poor substitute for a mirror, Morea did her best to
straighten her hair and check her makeup. A quick pat
warned her of a few loose tendrils at the back of her
neck, and a couple of the pins which held her French
twist seemed to be sliding. She tucked them back into
place and thought that perhaps it was a good thing that
Ridge Coltrain was oblivious to appearances.

After three years on the staff of Taylor Bradley
Cummings, Morea still thought that walking into the offices was like entering another universe. Even the air in
the reception room smelled like no other aroma on earth.
She could isolate a few of the scents—leather, old books,
a trace of expensive perfume—but in fact, Morea had

always thought, the overwhelming aroma was that of money.

She waved a casual hand at the receptionist and hurried down the wide, deep-carpeted hallway toward her own minisuite. In the outer office, her secretary held up a stack of pink message slips. "Do you want these or shall I hold them? Mr. Coltrain's already in your conference room."

"There is no justice in the universe," Morea grumbled. "Just once, why can't *he* be the one who's thirty seconds late? Give us two hours, Cindy, and then interrupt." She took the folder Cindy handed her and crossed to the closed door of her private conference room.

This room, even more than the engraved nameplate on her door, was Morea's favorite symbol of success. Her own conference room—not one shared with the rest of the practice. Not a place, as in many firms, which doubled as a lunchroom for staff or attorneys. In fact, there hadn't been a pizza box, a sandwich wrapper, or a soft-drink can allowed in this room since Morea's promotion.

The oval table in the center of the room was teak, its top inlaid with other contrasting woods in a subtle pattern. Six dark-green leather chairs were drawn up around it.

In one of them, with his back to the door, sat Ridge Coltrain. He didn't turn when she came in, but despite his stillness and the smooth, quiet motion of the door, Morea knew he was aware of her presence.

"Admiring my view?" she said calmly.

He didn't miss a beat. "Not only the view, but the ambience. I always wonder, though, what your clients think when they're ushered in here. Or don't they realize how much of their hourly fee goes to pay for leather and teak and Oriental rugs instead of good legal advice?"

His voice seemed to fill the room, wrapping her in its rich, unhurried softness. For the first time, she wondered if the note of lazy ease which always annoyed her so— was the man never in a hurry?—was, instead, the slightest remaining hint of a drawl. She knew very little about him, really.

And, she reminded herself, she had no desire to know more—apart from the things which might someday help her in a courtroom.

She followed his gaze toward the wide window and the Rocky Mountains far beyond the city, their outline slightly hazy today in the humid air of midsummer. "Don't worry about it, Ridge. Before we allow real clients in here, we always put on a paper tablecloth and bring in the bent-up folding chairs."

Ridge laughed and lazily uncoiled to his full height. "Good to see you, Morea—as always. Even when you're late."

After a dozen encounters, Morea thought, she ought not to react to him this way. But every time she saw him, it seemed she'd forgotten not only how tall he was—six inches taller than Morea even when she was wearing her highest heels—but how his mere presence in a room seemed to rearrange every molecule of air like iron filings falling into line around a magnet.

Ridge Coltrain wasn't handsome, exactly. His ears were slightly too big for masculine beauty, his golden-brown hair a little too uncontrolled. His suits were perfectly tailored, but his lean, rangy body made them look as if he bought his clothes off the rack anyway.

But there was something about the way he was put together that made him terribly easy to look at. Plus there was an air about him of solidity, self-confidence, and steadiness; the man appeared to be as reliable as the Rock of Gibraltar.

At least he looks that way if you're his client, Morea thought. Those same characteristics could strike terror into the heart of an opposing attorney, and she'd found out the hard way that appearances didn't lie. Ridge Coltrain was not only solid and self-assured, he was as tenacious as a pit bull. Above all, he was intelligent. His dark brown eyes were large and liquid and all-seeing...

And just what, Morea wondered, was he finding so fascinating about her today? She'd never seen that speculative look in his eyes before. He was looking her over as closely as if she was a product on the shelf and he a consumer considering whether to buy.

Was he working out some sort of new strategy on the Madison case and wondering if he could push it past her? Surely not; he'd no doubt listened to the same law school lectures she had. Besides, Ridge was far too experienced to let an opponent see the merest hint of uncertainty.

But what else could it be, if not the Madisons? There certainly couldn't be anything *personal* about this inspection; Morea's mouth went dry at the very idea, and she had to draw on long practice at self-control to watch him levelly as she moved around the table and sat down.

Her secretary brought in a tray with a china coffee pot and silently poured the dark rich fluid into two gold-trimmed cups and saucers. She placed one beside Ridge, then added a splash of cream to Morea's cup and set it by her elbow.

Wait a minute, Morea thought. He couldn't have been there long, or Cindy would already have given him coffee. So where did he get off nagging her about being late?

Ridge ignored his saucer and cradled the cup in his hand, his long fingers seeming to caress the hot, smooth china as he inhaled the steam. "Just the way I like it," he murmured.

"Well, maybe you can aspire to this sort of thing someday."

"China cups, Oriental rugs, and express elevators? And make all the compromises that go with those things?" He shook his head. "Oh, no. I'll just continue to suggest to my divorce clients that their soon-to-be-ex-partners hire you."

"Thanks," Morea said dryly.

The corner of his mouth quirked upward. "That way I can continue to drink your coffee, admire your view, park in a reserved spot, and not have to pay for it all myself."

And not feel intimidated by the opposition in court, either, Morea added to herself. But she refused to take the bait. Just because he'd beaten her once didn't mean she was incapable of returning the favor. "I noticed you'd traded cars."

"Did you? The convertible does stand out a bit, doesn't it?"

"Particularly when it's parked in that particular place."

"Don't be petty, Morea. I've never seen all those spots full at any given time, so why shouldn't I park there? The firm's paying the bill whether the spaces are in use or not. In fact, you should thank me."

"For what?"

"Doing my bit to make TBC look busy and success-ful." He leaned back in his chair. "So tell me, Counselor—has Kathy Madison decided yet to give up on the impossible quest and let Bill keep his business?"

Morea wasn't fooled by the casual note in his voice; it was perfectly clear that he was on the attack. She said sweetly, "Now that's a well-phrased question if I ever heard one, Mr. Coltrain, sir. It's something like that old classic, 'Have you stopped beating your dog?'"

He grinned. "And have you?"

"You know exactly what I mean, Ridge. No matter how I answer that question it leaves the wrong impression, so let me just restate our position. Kathy devoted as much time and work toward building that business as Bill did during their marriage, and she deserves her share." She flipped open the folder she'd brought in and held out a single sheet of paper. "Here's what we're proposing. This is only a summary, of course. The details will still have to be worked out."

He took the page, but he didn't look at it. He was still watching her, and Morea found it unnerving.

"If I have spinach stuck in my teeth," she said finally, "I'll be happy to excuse myself and remove it so you can concentrate on the business at hand."

Ridge smiled. "Why remove it? Wouldn't you rather keep me on edge and unable to focus?"

Uneasily, Morea wondered if there *was* something stuck in her teeth. Not spinach, of course; she hadn't eaten any in weeks. But since she hadn't had time to check her mirror...

"That's not what's on my mind anyway," he went on. "I was just wondering..." His voice trailed off as he glanced at the property settlement she'd handed him.

It's only a game he's playing, Morea told herself. She'd encountered the phenomenon before, of course; a good many male attorneys thought a sizzling stare at an attractive woman would render her unable to think. Ridge had just put his own spin on the technique, distracting her with the implication that there was something wrong with her appearance. He must be less certain of his ground on the Madisons' property settlement than she'd expected, to be playing that sort of game.

Determined to press her advantage, Morea settled back in her chair and began detailing the points in her summary. Ridge listened, appearing very patient, putting in a comment here and there. Now and then he shook his head and suggested a change, and after a while he took a fountain pen out of his shirt pocket and started to make additions all over his copy of her carefully constructed proposal.

Morea had no idea how much time had passed when her secretary came quietly into the room. "I'm sorry, Ms. Landon, but you asked me to remind you of your next appointment."

Ridge didn't look up from the changes he was scrawling in the margin. Much of the page was now covered with bold black ink.

"Thanks, Cindy." Morea glanced at the once-neat page with distaste. "I think we've done as much as we can this afternoon, don't you, Ridge?"

"I've certainly tried my best to reassure you of your job security." He capped his fountain pen and slid the agreement across the table to Morea.

She glanced at it and handed the page to the secretary. "Plug in these changes and additions, will you, Cindy? And get a copy to Mr. Coltrain this afternoon for him to review."

"Of course. Shall I messenger it over to your office, sir?"

"Not over," Ridge said. "Just down. My new office is on the eighth floor."

"In this building?" Morea started to gather up the contents of the Madisons' folder. "What prompted that move?"

"You mean you have to ask? Every important person in Denver knows which building Taylor Bradley Cummings is in, and my new letterhead—whenever I get around to ordering some—will have that same illustrious address."

The sparkle in his eyes warned Morea not to take him too seriously. "Are you sure you can stand the reflected glory?" she asked dryly.

"I'll try to rise to the challenge." Ridge pushed his chair back. "Run that proposal past Kathy as soon as you have a chance, and I'll talk to Bill, and then we can get them together and fine-tune it. Same time next week?"

The faintest possible edge in his voice made Morea glance at him through her lashes. The sparkle of humor was gone, and he once again looked watchful, almost wary, as he had at the beginning of the session. *Careful*, she thought suddenly. As if she represented danger...

She shrugged. "Fine-tune, or else start over."

"That's a cheap shot, Morea—not worthy of your talent."

She didn't argue, for he was right; it had been only a feeble effort. She flipped open her notebook calendar and nodded agreement. "I'll see you next Friday afternoon, then."

"Good. It's my turn to entertain, by the way." He smiled suddenly. "Sounds like I'm offering dinner and a movie, doesn't it?"

Morea almost shivered at the thought.

"Now that I have my new office, I'll show you how the rest of the legal world operates—the half that doesn't believe an attorney's quality is reflected in the cost of his office furniture."

"In that case," Morea murmured, "I'll bring my own chair."

Ridge stood up slowly and without apparent haste walked across to the door which led into Cindy's office and on toward the main reception room. "'Bye, Morea.

I'll look forward to next week—it's always so much fun fighting with you.''

The stack of pink message slips had doubled in the two hours she'd been closeted with Ridge Coltrain. Morea flipped through them, automatically sorting the calls by priority, fitting the slips together like a poker hand.

The calls represented the usual range of troubles encountered by an attorney who spent most of her time dealing with divorce and domestic situations—one client reported nonpayment of child support, another wanted to change her ex-husband's visitation schedule, a third needed a restraining order on a former boyfriend who'd turned obsessive and begun stalking her.

''I'm going to return these calls and then settle down to work on the Petrovsky case,'' she told Cindy. ''Her court date's next Thursday, isn't it?''

Her secretary nodded. ''Ten in the morning.''

Morea started toward her own office, and then turned back. ''Wait a minute,'' she said. ''Cindy, wasn't there some kind of message from my mother?''

''No. Why?''

''I ran into her in the parking garage. I thought she'd stopped in while I was gone to lunch.''

Cindy shook her head. ''I haven't even seen Meredith in close to a month.''

Morea frowned. ''Maybe she left a note with the receptionist and it hasn't gotten back here yet.''

''I'll check. But I doubt it—the girls up front are very careful with that sort of thing.''

That was true. ''Or maybe she realized how late it was and didn't bother to come all the way into the building.'' Morea shrugged. ''Hold all my calls, will you?''

In her office, she turned her big leather chair to the window. It wasn't the Rockies that she stared at, though, but the page still imprinted in her mind—Ridge's copy of the Madisons' property settlement, complete with his bold black additions and changes.

She ought to be working on Susan Petrovsky's case, Morea knew. There was plenty to be done on it before Thursday, and a half-dozen other cases waited in the wings, as well. But there was a particular challenge about the Madison case...

Be honest, she told herself. *You're terrified you've missed something—and you know Ridge Coltrain won't hesitate to use it.*

And if so, she'd better find it before she talked to Kathy Madison—and before it was too late to call Ridge Coltrain to account.

The house where Morea had grown up, in a middle-class neighborhood not far from the university where her father taught English literature, was one of the neatest in the block, a story-and-a-half brick cottage, surrounded by flowers, with a hanging swing on the tiny front porch. Morea thought it looked more and more like a dollhouse as the years passed.

Meredith Landon was kneeling by the front steps, weeding a flower bed, when Morea's BMW pulled into the drive on Sunday afternoon. Meredith stood up, stripping her dirt-stained gloves off, as Morea crossed the drive. "Hello, darling. How was the banquet last night?"

Morea shrugged. "Like most of these charity things. The after-dinner speaker labored under the illusion that the crowd actually wanted to hear him speak, so he went on for nearly an hour."

Meredith only nodded.

She looked tired, Morea thought suddenly, and there were new, tiny stress lines around her mother's dark eyes. Dread closed around Morea's chest like an iron band. She'd sensed something different about Meredith that day in the parking garage, but there hadn't been time to think about it then, and in the press of work she'd forgotten all about it. Now she felt awful; how could she have overlooked something so obvious? Why hadn't she called her mother Friday night, as she'd planned?

Because you were still hitting the books at midnight, she reminded herself. And it wasn't as if Meredith needed a keeper, anyway. She was perfectly capable of asking for help if she needed it.

Which was probably why she'd called yesterday and asked Morea to stop by...

"I'm sorry I couldn't come last night, Mom."

Meredith shrugged. "It's all right, darling. After thirty years in a university community, I know how these things work. You're here now, and that's what matters." She tossed her gloves down into the rich loam of the flower bed and glanced, with a frown, toward the house.

Morea caught the look. "What's wrong? Is Daddy all right?"

"He's napping this afternoon."

That's really not an answer, Morea wanted to say. But she bit her tongue. Part of her didn't want to hear what Meredith might say. Charles Landon wasn't young anymore; he was only a few years from retirement.

"Shall we sit in the swing for a while?" Meredith asked. "It's such a pretty day, I hate to go inside."

And risk waking Daddy, Morea added, to herself. She followed Meredith onto the porch and settled quietly by her mother's side in the old wooden swing. The chains which held it protested as Meredith pushed the swing into motion, and then settled into a creaky, hypnotic lullaby.

Morea stayed silent.

Finally Meredith sighed. "I'm glad it worked out this way, actually. Having a chance to talk to you alone, I mean."

"Is Daddy ill?"

"No—not actually. But... Morea, he doesn't want you to know anything about this. So please, darling, you have to promise me..."

"I don't like to play that game, Mother." But Meredith's lips set firmly into line, as if she was fully prepared to say not another word, and finally Morea gave in. "All right—you tell me what's going on, and I'll promise that I won't bring it up to him without warning you first. Fair enough?"

"If that's all I can get, I'll take it," Meredith said. "Some days I regret sending you to law school, Morea." But the humor in her eyes was strained, and it quickly died away. "Charles has been working with a young woman in his department for some time. She's a doctoral candidate, and he's one of her committee of advisors."

Morea nodded. Most of the time, she knew, Charles was working with half a dozen such students.

"Her work hasn't been up to standard," Meredith went on, "and Charles has tried his best to keep her from failing. Extra help, extra conferences...but it hasn't worked out, and finally he had to recommend that she be dropped from the program and her teaching fellowship terminated."

There was nothing unusual about the story so far, Morea knew. Not every doctoral candidate was successful, and though it was quite like her tenderhearted father to give each one the benefit of every doubt, there came a time when even Charles Landon had to give up.

Meredith wet her lips. "She responded by filing a complaint against him."

"Against *Daddy*?"

"For sexual harassment. She says that her work was only found to be substandard because she turned down his advances."

"*Daddy*?" Morea felt like a broken record.

Meredith nodded. "The university has to investigate, of course. It'll be public record—"

"He doesn't want to tell me, so he was going to let me read it on the front page of the Denver *Post*?"

Meredith went straight on as if she hadn't heard. "Unless he simply resigns. Then the investigation will be dropped, and—"

Morea shook her head. "Oh, no. We're going to fight this."

"He doesn't want to, Morea."

"Mother, it's his reputation at stake!"

"I know that, darling—and so does he. That's exactly why he doesn't want to fight. He believes the publicity would damage his reputation far more than a quiet resignation. He could say it was for health reasons, and—"

"Well, he's wrong. I mean, the publicity won't help, but to quit without a fight is admitting to the charge. He might as well write a confession!"

"You don't have to convince me. I agree with you, Morea—I want him to fight it, too. But you know your father. He can be the gentlest, sweetest, most absent-minded and malleable of men. But when he feels his principles are involved..."

Morea knew. She'd encountered that side of her father more often in her teenage years than she cared to remember. "But they *are* involved," she said stubbornly. "And he should want to fight to preserve his good name. All right—what are we going to do?" The question was addressed more to herself than to her mother.

"He's agreed to talk to an attorney," Meredith said. Her voice held an odd note that honed Morea's curiosity. "I must say I'd like to know how you managed that," she admitted. "Not that it matters just now. We'll get the best. I'll have to ask around the practice for recommendations, but we'll find out who has experience with harassment cases. And defamation suits, too, perhaps—"

"A specific attorney."

Morea blinked. "I didn't know Daddy knew any. Except me, of course."

"He doesn't, really—he just knows of him."

"Oh, now that's a really intelligent way to choose the man he's going to trust his life to!"

"That's why I'm confiding in you, Morea."

"You want me to talk Daddy out of it?" In the next breath Morea answered her own question. "No, it can't be that—not if Daddy thinks I don't even know about this whole business. If it's the attorney you want me to talk to, to persuade him not to take the case because you want someone else... I don't know, Mom. That's really touchy ethical ground."

"I want you to talk him into helping us."

Morea didn't answer. Above her head, the chains of the swing rasped and grated.

"I went to talk to him, you see," Meredith said softly. "He said he won't take the case."

Relief trickled through Morea's veins. "Then you're better off with someone else. If this guy doesn't believe in Daddy—"

"He's the only one Charles will even talk to, I'm sure of that. It's either that, or Charles will resign. And there isn't much time, Morea. He's already written his resignation letter. He's only held off sending it because I pleaded and cried."

Morea's heart sank. The idea of her serene, calm, always-in-control mother pleading for what she felt was right, of her father turning his back on a career he loved because of a hurtful falsehood, made her ache all over.

Meredith was staring straight ahead. Her voice was flat, as if she knew that this was the last card in her hand and the outcome was already decided. "Will you talk to the lawyer, Morea? Persuade him that he's the only one Charles might be able to trust?"

That was a strange way of putting it, Morea thought. "All right. I'll try."

Meredith reached into the pocket of her jeans. "Here's his card. Well, not his card, exactly, he didn't have one."

Despite the warmth of the summer breeze, Morea's blood chilled as abruptly as if she'd been dunked in a tank of ice water. "Who?" she said.

"Ridge Coltrain," Meredith said. "I think he's the nicest young man. So straightforward and trustworthy and *solid*. Don't you agree, Morea?"

CHAPTER TWO

MOREA could have bitten off her tongue. *Never commit yourself to a course of action for a client before you've considered all the consequences*, one of her professors had said. But because this particular client happened to be her mother, she'd walked into a rat's nest.

She closed her eyes in pain, and as if on a movie screen she once again saw Meredith, soberly dressed in a neat suit, coming out of the skywalk entrance of Morea's own building—the building where Ridge Coltrain had established his new office. No wonder Meredith hadn't been chatty that afternoon. No wonder she hadn't left a message for Morea...

"Oh, great," Morea said. She didn't even attempt to keep the sarcasm out of her voice. "And just what makes Daddy so sure Ridge is the one to save him?"

"I didn't exactly say that, Morea."

Morea wasn't listening. "Because Ridge beat me in the Simmons case last year, is that it?"

"Well," Meredith said reasonably, "he must be good in order to pull that off."

"That is the single most backhanded compliment I've ever received in my life, Mother." Morea cleared her throat. After all, she reminded herself, Meredith was under a great deal of strain just now. And, even though Morea felt her promise had been extracted under duress, she *had* promised.

"All right," she said grudgingly. "I'll talk to Ridge."

Relief flickered across Meredith's face. "If you can just convince him to meet Charles, talk to him—"

"Now wait a minute. Are you saying Ridge won't even *talk* to Daddy?"

Meredith looked away, and abruptly the stress was back in her face. "Well, there hasn't really been an opportunity. I went by myself to see him, just to get his opinion, and—"

Morea said, levelly, "You went without telling Daddy." It wasn't a question.

"I didn't believe there was any point in telling Charles until I knew what Ridge had to say. But Ridge seemed to think perhaps he shouldn't get involved—"

"And he's got some reason. Because of the other case we're litigating, this could be considered a conflict of interest. Particularly," Morea added dryly, "when I go beg him to take it on."

"Oh. I hadn't thought of that, exactly."

"And I can understand why he wouldn't exactly be eager to sign on with a client who's so reluctant he doesn't even come in himself." She sighed. "I'll talk to him, Mother. But I can't promise anything."

Meredith didn't answer. That surprised Morea, who had half expected some sign of gratitude. Of course, there was nothing to thank her for yet—and perhaps there wasn't going to be.

The swing creaked, the chain groaned, and Meredith said, "I suppose I'd better tell you the rest."

Foreboding inched up Morea's spine. "The rest of what?"

"Charles still doesn't know I went to see Ridge."

"You mean—wait a minute. I thought you said Daddy agreed to talk to him."

"He did. Just not about the case."

"Mother, so help me—"

Meredith took a deep breath. "I told Charles you wanted him to meet Ridge, because you think he's very special and that he might be the one you want to spend your life with.''

Morea exploded from the swing, wheeled around to face her mother, and planted both hands on her hips. *"You told Daddy I'm in love with Ridge Coltrain?"*

"Not exactly. I certainly didn't say there was anything agreed between you. I just hinted that you thought…" She obviously noted the thunderous fury in Morea's face, and her voice trailed off.

And perhaps that, Morea thought, explained why Ridge had looked at her on Friday afternoon as if she were a deadly microbe. Though surely Meredith hadn't told him all of this—had she?

"Oh, Morea, don't you see? If Charles knows this is all about the harassment charge, he'll clam up and that will be the end of it. But if he can meet Ridge in a social situation and start to trust him—''

"So invite Ridge to the next faculty tea!''

"If you introduce him, Charles will start out wanting to like Ridge, and wanting Ridge to like him—''

"I wouldn't bet any money on it. Daddy's never seemed too thrilled about the guys I've dated.''

"That was when you were a teenager, Morea.''

"Exactly. Why do you think I haven't brought any men around to meet him since I grew up?''

"That's precisely why having you bring Ridge to dinner will make Charles relax and be himself.''

"Dinner? Why don't you just invite us for the weekend?''

Meredith looked shocked. "Morea—we only have one guest room.''

"My point exactly. If you want to convince Daddy we're serious.… Oh, never mind. Mother, this has to be the craziest, most mixed-up scheme I've ever heard of, and if you think I'm going to participate—''

Meredith's voice was quiet. "Would you rather your father just quietly resign and break his heart over it?"

Morea's annoyance drained away, leaving her almost as light-headed as if it was blood spilling from her body. "No. Of course not." She straightened her shoulders. "All right, Mother, I'll try."

Morea didn't wait for the end of her father's nap. The last thing she wanted to do was face Charles Landon before she'd had a chance to think this whole thing through and decide what her role was to be.

She was headed for her apartment, in one of Denver's newer residential towers, when she realized that she didn't have the luxury of time to think. Between her work schedule for the next week and the little she knew of Ridge's, she might have to spend days playing telephone tag in order to catch him—days she couldn't afford to lose. She could, of course, wait till their appointment on Friday, but by then Charles might have submitted his resignation and the whole question would be moot.

She pulled off the wide boulevard into the nearest parking lot, fumbling for her car phone and the bulky telephone book which she kept stuffed under the passenger seat. Maybe she could catch Ridge at home right now.

Ridge wasn't listed, but there was a Richard and an R.L. On principle, she tried the initials first. Besides, she thought, with a tinge of cynicism, it was an address which sounded like Ridge—a middle-class neighborhood right next door to one of the best areas of the city.

A woman answered, and Morea said, "Excuse me, I'm sorry to bother you. I'm trying to reach Ridge Coltrain, the attorney, and I wondered if you could help me."

The woman's voice was pleasant, warm and clear. "I'm afraid he's not here."

Morea almost dropped the phone. "You mean—he lives there?"

The warmth drained out of the voice. "As of this morning, yes. May I ask who's calling?"

"Oh—I'm sorry. I'm Morea Landon. I'm also an attorney."

"I believe he's mentioned you. May I take a message?"

"I need to talk to him as soon as possible."

"In that case, why don't you go over to his office? He said he'd be there most of the day."

"I'll do that. Thank you—" Morea hesitated. *Ma'am* didn't seem quite appropriate, but what else was she to call the woman?

"Mrs. Coltrain," the warm voice supplied, and a dial tone sounded in Morea's ear.

Mrs. Coltrain? Ridge didn't wear a wedding ring...

But he did wear a gold signet on his left hand, she remembered, with his initials embossed on the flat top. It was odd, but she hadn't even realized till now that she'd noticed the ring, much less paid attention to its design.

The habit of observation, she told herself. She'd had a professor who'd harped on the importance of such details; she just hadn't realized how deeply his lectures had taken root.

Why hadn't it occurred to her that signets could be wedding rings? And why should she be so surprised that Ridge was married? Just because he'd always seemed to her to be the type to remain footloose in private life...

Boy, is my mother going to be disappointed at this news, Morea reflected. If Meredith *had* told Ridge the details of her plan, no wonder he hadn't wanted to be involved!

She started to look up his office number, then remembered his recent move. In any case, she decided, even if his phone number hadn't changed, this was the sort of thing best handled in person.

Ridge's convertible was parked in what was apparently his favorite place, the first spot in the row Taylor Bradley Cummings reserved for clients.

Don't make a fuss, Morea told herself. Nobody else used the spots on Sunday, so it was no big deal if Ridge did—even if it did appear that he was thumbing his nose at the entire firm, and at Morea in particular.

She parked the BMW two spaces away, leaving plenty of room between its spotless silver paint and the slightly piebald convertible, and dug for her key to the skywalk door. For the first time she remembered that she was hardly dressed for a professional conference in her jeans and running shoes and lightweight white cotton sweater. Well, Ridge probably wouldn't notice—and even if he did, perhaps he'd chalk it up to the importance of the situation.

Apart from the penthouse offices of Taylor Bradley Cummings and the gym in the sub-basement, she was less than familiar with the layout of the building. Plus she'd forgotten to take the slip of paper Meredith had waved at her, which had presumably included the number of Ridge's office suite.

Was it the eighth floor Ridge had said his new office was on? She checked the directory in the elevator lobby, but his name wasn't on the list yet. She started to make a systematic circle of the entire floor, checking each office till she found a small sign scrawled in familiar black ink and taped to a door.

The door wasn't locked, and she pushed it open gently

to see a waiting room which contained a desk, a filing cabinet, and a single straight chair. "Ridge? Are you here?"

Something creaked, and Ridge appeared in the doorway across the room. "Well, if it isn't Morea." He leaned against the jamb and folded his arms across his chest.

It was a broader chest than she'd realized before, Morea noticed. Or did it just look broader because of the bold stripe of his casual short-sleeved shirt? She'd never seen him without a suit jacket before, and the way the muscles in his arms flexed as he moved startled her. And then there was the way his well-worn jeans clung to his body...

"You don't sound surprised to see me," she said.

"Actually, I am. I was hoping for one of those peroxide blondes who always show up in the first chapter of private-investigator novels. But I guess you'll have to do."

"You're not a private investigator, Ridge."

He snapped his fingers. "Maybe that's where I've gone wrong! What can I do for you? Is there something new on the Madison home front?"

Morea shook her head. Since she didn't want to conduct this conversation while standing, and since there was only one chair in the waiting room, she tried to slip past him and into the inner office. The doorway was standard size, but with him occupying half of it, her shoulder brushed his folded arms, and the warmth of his body seemed to scorch her side.

His eyebrows lifted, and there was a wry note in his voice. "Come in and make yourself comfortable."

"Thanks." Morea surveyed the office. A plain wooden desk, nicely kept but nothing memorable, occupied the center of the room, with a well-worn leather armchair behind it. A half-dozen bookshelves had been added to one long wall, and a stack of empty boxes nearby bore witness to the work he'd been doing. She settled into the armchair which was drawn up primly in front of his desk, and winced. "Though I'd say *comfortable* is an overstatement. I'll definitely bring my own chair on Friday."

Ridge walked around the desk and sat down. His chair tipped back alarmingly, echoing the creak she'd heard when she called his name. "It's amazing how quickly people come to the point when they're sitting in that chair."

She watched as he swept papers into a folder and set it aside. She didn't recall noticing how long his hands were and how well-shaped, but she must have—there was a familiarity about the graceful way he moved.

"Of course," Ridge went on, "at your hourly rate, you probably don't mind how long your clients chat."

"I can take a hint, Ridge." She shifted, trying to achieve a little more comfort. "You could have told me you've met my mother."

"Client privilege." Ridge shrugged. "I shouldn't have to explain to you that if I talked about who's been pouring her heart out in my office, I'd be in hot water with the bar."

"Pouring her heart out?"

"Rhetorically speaking," he added smoothly. "Can I assume that she's told you what's going on? Because I can't, you know."

"She filled me in on the high spots, at any rate. A student has it in for Daddy, and the college wants him to resign rather than risk a fuss." She paused, half-hoping that despite what he'd said he'd volunteer to fill in the blanks, but Ridge only nodded. "She says you turned down the case," Morea went on.

"Wouldn't you have? Under the circumstances—"

Morea wondered precisely which circumstances he was talking about. The facts of the case itself? Charles' reluctance to seek help? Or Meredith's incredible plan to persuade her husband?

Morea pushed that last thought away. "I understand, of course, why this kind of case wouldn't be quite your style."

"Do you?" Ridge murmured.

"That's why I have a proposal for you."

"Somehow I expected you'd have a few ideas of your own." He leaned back even farther, till his chair looked as if it were defying gravity, and laced his fingers together atop his belt buckle.

Morea watched the chair with fascination and finally had to drag her attention back to the problem at hand. "Mother thinks if you'd just meet with Daddy, you could convince him to fight. If you'll do that much, I'll take care of finding the best attorney in Colorado to actually represent him—somebody who's experienced with defamation and sexual harassment suits. You wouldn't have to be involved in the case itself at all."

"Why stop with Colorado?" He stared at the ceiling. "Go for the best in the nation."

"It was a figure of speech, Coltrain. Of course I'll get the best there is. This is my father, after all."

He nodded thoughtfully. "I knew my confidence in you wasn't misplaced, Morea. But you know, it's still not an easy assignment you want me to take on. I got the impression that Charles will only make an appearance in this office if your mother confines him in a straitjacket."

Morea looked down at her hands, folded almost casually in her lap. Her white knuckles, however, were a dead giveaway. This wasn't going to be easy; if

Meredith had confided her plan to Ridge, Morea was going to look and feel like a fool for tiptoeing around the subject. If Meredith hadn't told him what she had in mind, he might think it was Morea's idea instead— which would be even worse.

She took a deep breath. "Mother thinks if you were to meet him in a social situation, he'd be more likely to develop enough trust to confide in you and take your advice."

"Hmm. That's an interesting approach."

Morea waited, but he obviously wasn't going to say any more. She decided it was time to bite the bullet. "She wants you to come to dinner."

"Really? And I suppose she'll casually mention that her new friend just happens to be an attorney, expecting that Charles won't get suspicious?"

Morea groaned inwardly. So Meredith hadn't confided her entire scheme. *Gee, thanks, Mom*, she thought, *for leaving it up to me*. "Well, she wants to tell him that you and I...that you and I are..." She couldn't look at him. "That we're dating."

Ridge abruptly sat up straight, his chair groaning in protest as if every nail was being slowly and simultaneously yanked out. There was honest amazement in his face, the first Morea had ever seen there. "No," he said. "You're joking. You and me? *Dating*?" He started to laugh.

He didn't need to be quite so highly amused at the idea, Morea thought indignantly. It wasn't *that* incredibly funny. Of course, she reminded herself, there was the wife. Maybe she should be glad he wasn't taking it seriously.

"I know," she said crisply. "It makes no sense whatever, and anybody who was thinking clearly would never have come up with such a wet-noodle idea. But I'm sure you noticed that my mother isn't thinking terribly clearly these days. Also, I wouldn't put it past her to have already told Daddy all about it.''

"Well, I hope she hasn't set the wedding date just yet," Ridge mused. He rubbed long fingers along his jaw. "It might be a bit awkward."

Sarcasm dripped from Morea's voice. "That occurred to you, did it? I always knew you were an incisive thinker, Ridge.''

"Especially if one or the other of us is supposed to be in divorce court that day instead. As ideas go, though, it's just crazy enough that it might work."

Morea tried to freeze him with a stare. "Well, I suppose we could play along with her idea for a while. At least it gives me the perfect excuse for breaking off our supposed relationship as soon as you've accomplished your purpose. All I have to do is 'discover' that you misled me about your wife, go cry on my father's shoulder, and—"

"What wife?"

"What do you mean, what wife? I just talked to her. She's the one who sent me over here."

Ridge grinned. She'd never noticed before how his eyes came to life when he was amused. "Oh, *that* wife."

"Have you considered maybe you're working too hard these days, Coltrain?"

"Why? You trying to get me to lighten up on Kathy Madison?" He didn't wait for an answer. "So, Ms. Landon—what's in this for me? So far, it sounds like a thankless cause."

"Think how good you'll feel," Morea said, "helping to save a man's career."

"Ah. Of course, feeling good doesn't pay the electric bill."

"You mean you actually pay it?"

"Only because I can't find an extension cord long enough to run all the way up to TBC's floor."

Morea didn't know why she bothered to spar with him; the man was never short of an answer. "All right, Ridge, what kind of fee do you want?"

"I'll think it over and let you know," he said promptly.

Suspicion flooded through her. "Perhaps I should remind you that my parents aren't exactly well off," she began. "And though I expect to pick up a good share of the bill for this, I'm not precisely wealthy, either."

"A TBC attorney who's not wealthy? My sympathies, darling. But that's all right—I'm sure you have all sorts of assets," Ridge said mildly. "By the way, when's this special dinner coming off, so I can clear my calendar? And is Charles the kind who'll be impressed if I bring your mother candy and flowers, or do you think that's overdoing it?"

Taylor Bradley Cummings' executive dining room had never been Morea's favorite place to lunch. The food was good, if a bit on the bland side in order to suit the palates of the most elderly senior partners, but going there wasn't like escaping to the outer world. She'd much rather call up a friend and meet at the Pinnacle.

Today, however, Morea had good reason to stay close to the practice. She deliberately waited till most of her partners were already at lunch before she strolled down to the dining room, selected a salad from the buffet bar, and looked around the room.

She waved at a couple of the younger senior partners but didn't move to join them. They both specialized in business mergers and acquisitions, and therefore weren't likely to have the information she needed. A couple of the men she'd been hoping to find weren't there; they must have gone out for lunch. Well, if she had to seek them out in their offices, she would—it was just that she'd so much rather make the contact, and ask her question, casually...

At a table nearby, a blond man in a dark blue pin-striped suit leaped up and gestured toward her, holding the chair next to his.

Morea gave a deep inward sigh, but she couldn't be so actively rude as to ignore the invitation. Alan Davis was a good sort; he'd joined the firm just a short while before Morea herself, and he'd helped her learn the ropes in her first weeks on the job. Of course, after that it had taken the better part of a year to convince him that she felt so strongly about mixing business with pleasure that she'd never date a partner. In fact, she wasn't absolutely certain that he'd got the message yet.

She set her salad down. "Hi, Alan."

He held her chair and reseated himself with a flurry. "I haven't seen you in weeks, Morea. Has the firm got that many divorces going on right now?"

"Along with prenuptial agreements, adoptions, rene-gotiations of child support, domestic abuse cases..."

"Oh. I guess I forgot all those other things fell into your domain, too. I'm sending one of my clients over to see you, by the way. He's considering divorce and needs some advice on how to get out of the marriage without it costing him a bundle."

"Does he have kids?"

"At least one. Why?"

"Then it *ought* to cost him a bundle," Morea said crisply. "But of course I'll talk to him—and the sooner the better."

Alan nodded. "I know what you mean. Before his wife gets suspicious and hires some hotshot of her own.

Speaking of hotshots—you're going up against Ridge Coltrain again, aren't you?''

"Don't remind me." Morea stabbed a bit of lettuce and then thought better of the comment. "Why? Do you know something I should be aware of?"

Alan shrugged. "Nope. All I know is he seems to have come out of nowhere. He's only been around Denver for a year or so."

Interesting, Morea thought. She'd never thought to ask; she'd assumed Ridge had always practiced in Denver, and hadn't even considered why she had never encountered him before the Simmons case. It must have been one of the first he'd handled, though, if he'd been in the city just a year.

Alan went on, "And he's good."

"*That* I already knew," Morea said dryly.

"He really whipped you a while back, didn't he?"

"On the Simmons case? I wouldn't call it a whipping, exactly. The court had to make a choice on custody, and my client lost."

"And you haven't gotten over the sting of it yet, have you? The longer you practice, the more you'll get used to that sort of thing, Morea. Win a few, lose a few."

A heavy hand landed on Alan's shoulder, and George Bradley, one of the founding partners, boomed, "I hope I'm interrupting a business conference!" He laughed heartily at his own joke and pulled out a chair. "You two are going to the bar association banquet that's coming up this month, aren't you?"

"Of course," Alan said smoothly. "In fact, I'd just asked Morea if she'd like to go with me."

"Good, good," Bradley said. "Keep it all in the family, right? I'll have my secretary bring the tickets around this afternoon, and you can give her a check for them." He started to rise.

"George," Morea said quickly. "I need your opinion on a referral, if you have a minute."

Bradley settled back into his chair. "Always happy to help, my dear."

"Who's the best person you know to try a defamation suit? And also, who's the best at defending against charges of sexual harassment? Not just in Colorado, either—I mean anywhere."

From the corner of her eye, she saw Alan's eyebrows raise.

Bradley rubbed the back of his hand across his jaw. "I should think Les McDonald, out of Seattle," he said finally. "If he's available, of course. He's not taking many cases these days. Or maybe—there was a big defamation case in Los Angeles a while back. Was it Carey who handled that one? I can't remember. Tell you what, I'll ask around and get back to you." He slapped Alan on the shoulder again. "Shall I send both those tickets to you, my boy?"

"I'll pay for my own," Morea said hastily.

Bradley winked at Alan. "One of the benefits of liberated women, eh?" he asked, and strolled across the room to another table of junior partners.

"Now there," Morea said under her breath, "is a real life male chauvinist—so oblivious he doesn't even realize what he is."

Alan laughed. "I don't think I'd care to be the one to confront him about it, but if you decide to, Morea, let me know. I'd love to have a front-row seat."

"I could sell tickets to that easier than to the bar association banquet. Darn it, it's almost blackmail—having the senior partners peddling tickets. Who's going to say no to George Bradley? We all just meekly fork over the fifty bucks and go."

"I'd like to take you, Morea."

"Thanks—but you know I have a rule about dating partners."

He looked dissatisfied. "Who *do* you date, then?"

Morea wondered what he'd say if she told him she was taking Ridge Coltrain home to officially meet her parents that very evening.

Suddenly her salad didn't taste as good, and she pushed it away and glanced at her watch. "I have to get back to work, Alan. My next client is due."

The statement was true enough, if perhaps a bit exaggerated; Kathy Madison's appointment was still half an hour away, but Morea planned to spend that time in one last perusal of the property settlement.

Kathy, however, was already in the waiting room when Morea reached her office suite. "I know I'm early," she said, standing up. "But I thought if you could fit me in, I wouldn't have to miss quite so much work."

"Of course. Come on in." Kathy had just started toward Morea's private office when the telephone on the secretary's desk chimed discreetly.

Cindy picked it up, shot a look at Kathy, whose back was turned, and gestured frantically at Morea. Then she cupped her hand over the mouthpiece. "It's Ridge Coltrain," she said under her breath.

Morea wanted to growl. The man's timing was absolutely incredible. But it would be foolish to refuse to take the call, in case it concerned the property settlement.

Besides, despite the low tone of Cindy's voice, Kathy had heard the name. "You mean, Bill's attorney?"

"The very one," Morea said. "Why don't you go on into my office, and I'll be there as soon as I find out what he wants?"

But Kathy didn't take the hint. She settled against the

side of Morea's office door as if prepared to stand there all day.

Morea could hardly order her to leave; it was Kathy's case, after all, and she had every right to hear what was going on. She reached across Cindy's desk to take the telephone. "Hello, Ridge."

"Morea, darling, I got your message about our dinner tonight. Shall I take your mother roses or some other kind of flower?"

"I hardly think it matters."

"Of course it matters. If she hates them, I'll look bad. And you certainly wouldn't want that, would you?"

Morea said, carefully, "In that case, the others, I think."

"Do I deduce you have someone in your office so you can't talk openly?"

"That's about the size of it."

He chuckled. "Oh, this could be fun."

"I'll have to call you back about that, Ridge."

"No, you don't. I won't torment you. Not today, anyway. Who's the important client, anyway? Or is it one of the partners?"

"Mrs. Madison and I are just discussing the property settlement now."

"What took you so long to show it to her, Morea? Have you been studying it all this time? Tell you what, since dinner's at seven—"

"That's right."

"Let's meet for a drink beforehand—sort of a dress rehearsal. Name the place and time."

Morea sighed. She'd agree to anything, she thought, just to get him off the telephone. "If you insist. Maxie's Bar, half past five."

"See you there, darling."

"Don't call me—" She stopped dead, but it was already too late; Kathy Madison looked quite intrigued. "I prefer Ms. Landon," she added crisply.

"Oh, wait till your father hears that," Ridge murmured, and hung up.

She'd have liked to run through her entire repertoire of swear words, but she counted to ten instead and then turned to Kathy with a determined smile. "Ridge," she said, "is quite the comedian. Unfortunately, it doesn't make him less effective as an attorney."

Kathy didn't answer. She appeared very thoughtful, and Morea didn't blame her. It didn't take a Mensa membership to figure out there'd been something distinctly odd about that conversation.

She ushered Kathy into her office and handed her the new version of the property settlement to review. Kathy read it slowly and finally looked up in disappointment. "But this—"

"I know it isn't what you'd hoped for," Morea said gently. "But as we've discussed, it's just about what I've expected all along, and we do have to be realistic. The business has great potential for growth, but dividing up the assets at this point would probably mean it wouldn't survive at all. However, if you accept a minority silent partnership—"

Kathy's brows drew together stubbornly. "A *silent* partnership would leave Bill free to run the place into the ground, and I couldn't say a word about it."

"Why would he do that? It's to his advantage for it to survive, too."

Kathy shook her head. "Why not let *him* have the silent partnership, then? I can run that business just as well as he can. I've been doing it for five years."

"But the origin of the business was his idea and his product."

"And my sweat and effort."

"That's true," Morea said gently. "And because of that we can make a good case for you to get a share. But I'm very much afraid that if we push this question to a court case, Bill will get the entire business."

Kathy was silent. Finally, she said, "This is really the best you think we can do?"

Morea nodded. "On the business, yes, but in return for your cooperation on that matter, I'm sure we can get a more generous share of his pension plan and the stock portfolio for you. So in sheer dollar terms—"

Kathy looked reluctant.

"It's all detailed in here," Morea said. "Perhaps you'd like to take this home and look it over at your leisure. Think about anything else you'd like to ask for, and call me if you have any questions. Can you come in on Friday for a conference with Bill and Ridge? Perhaps we can finalize this and move on."

Kathy nodded.

Morea walked her to the office door. The moment Kathy was out of earshot, Cindy said, "I'm really sorry. I only bothered you with that call because I thought it was something to do with the settlement."

Morea shrugged. "It can't be helped now."

"I know—but I feel bad, since it was obviously private. What's the deal with you and Ridge Coltrain, anyway?"

"I can't begin to explain," Morea said. "Mostly because I don't understand it myself. When I figure it out, Cindy, I'll let you know."

"Which is legalese, meaning you don't want to discuss it," Cindy muttered. "All I can say is, I never thought I'd see the day when a TBC attorney would be discussing property settlements with Ridge Coltrain at Maxie's Bar."

Neither did I, Morea thought. *Property settlements—
or anything else.*

But she had a sinking feeling that this anomaly would
be only the beginning.

CHAPTER THREE

MOREA was running late, and Ridge was waiting for her when she arrived at Maxie's, though it took her a while to find him. He'd chosen the most inaccessible corner of the dimly lit bar instead of a table in the restaurant section. Morea only saw him because a tiny spotlight which should have been focused on the dance floor happened to be turned at an angle which cast a golden highlight over his hair as he sat toying with a cellophane-wrapped sheaf of flowers.

If he'd been planning to make this encounter look like a date, she reflected, he couldn't have done any better.

He'd seen her, though, and he stood up, smiling, as she approached the table.

"Couldn't you have found any more intimate a location, Ridge?" she asked irritably.

"You chose the place." Ridge took the seat next to hers.

"I didn't tell you to hide in the darkest corner." Morea bent to slide her handbag under her chair. Her hair swept forward over her shoulder, so the first warning she had that Ridge was leaning toward her was when his hand casually scooped the silky mass back from her face. Even then, she had no inkling of his intentions until his lips brushed her cheek.

She sat back as if she'd been burned—and indeed she felt she had. Her skin seemed to sizzle where he'd touched her. "What was that all about?"

Ridge shrugged. "A hello kiss. What's the matter?

You were leaning over toward me as if you expected it.''

Morea's indignation warred with her common sense. It had been an idiotic thing for him to do, of course, but she'd seen the same kind of casual greeting in a hundred social settings, and even in some business ones. Fussing over it would only make the situation worse. Still, she was darned if she'd let him start that kind of nonsense.

''Well, don't get in the habit,'' she said. Ridge looked intrigued, and in pure self-defense Morea added, ''Or hasn't anyone warned you that I'm a rampant feminist and I take objection to things like that?''

Ridge's voice was soft. ''I'm sorry. I promise never to do it again.''

There was a sparkle in his eyes, however, which denied the penitence in his voice, and Morea decided that fact accounted for the flat, empty feeling in the pit of her stomach. The man was obviously up to something...

Or, whispered the tiny voice of conscience, did she feel a bit disappointed—and even guilty—because, fleeting and casual as that caress had been, she'd actually sort of liked it?

Absolutely not, she told herself. Because she *hadn't*.

''I hope those flowers aren't for me,'' she said crisply.

Ridge stroked the silky petal of an orange lily. ''Of course not. I brought them in so they wouldn't wilt in the heat of the car. Do you think your mother will like them?''

''I'm sure she'll be duly impressed with the gesture.'' Morea looked around for the waitress and beckoned her over to order a club soda. ''Daddy, on the other hand, may not even notice.''

Ridge leaned back in his chair, long fingers curled around his glass. ''Go on.''

''About my parents? What do you want to know?''

"If I could answer that, I wouldn't need to ask. What would you tell me if this meeting tonight was real?"

Morea shook her head. "This entire idea is insane, you know. The last person on earth my father would choose to confide in is someone he thinks I'm dating."

"Would you care to make a little bet of it?"

"Feeling particularly arrogant today, Coltrain?"

"It wouldn't be the first time you've underestimated me."

"If you're talking about the Simmons case," Morea said firmly, "that had nothing to do with our respective skills. She'd have gotten custody no matter who was arguing for or against her."

"And despite the fact that in every case since you've managed to fight me to a draw, you're still bent out of shape about Simmons versus Simmons, aren't you, darling? Oh—sorry. You did ask me not to call you that. So what would you like to bet?"

"I wouldn't."

Ridge shook his head sadly. "I never thought lack of confidence was one of your handicaps, Morea." He sipped his drink. "How about a steak dinner, winner's choice of locations?"

"How about getting down to business?"

"But that's what I meant, sweetheart. Or did you think I was suggesting we call it a date?"

Morea bit her tongue hard and told herself that nicknames were not worth arguing about; he no doubt had an inexhaustible supply. And as for the question of dating him...*that* wasn't even a suitable subject for comment. Even if he wasn't married, he was the last man on earth she'd be interested in.

Though he certainly didn't act married, Morea thought. On the other hand, if she was silly enough to say anything of the sort, she could almost hear his answer. *But precious, how does one act married? Would you care to show me?*

A shiver ran up her spine at the idea. No, she was infinitely better off keeping her mouth shut instead of challenging his behavior. Giving him a dose of his own medicine, though, if the opportunity arose—that was something else.

"You were saying something about your father being a bit oblivious," Ridge went on helpfully.

Relieved, Morea plunged in. "Not really. I mean, he's not exactly the absentminded professor, he's just a bit naive about the world sometimes. That's why I can really understand him getting into this trouble by trying to help a student."

"And perhaps the help was misunderstood?"

She thought about it. "I think it's more likely that Daddy was operating on good intentions and he just assumed everyone else was, too."

"But the student wasn't?" Ridge frowned. "It's possible, I suppose. You might find out all you can about that student."

"Why me?"

He smiled. "Because I'm not officially on the case—remember?" He glanced at his watch. "If we're going to be on time..."

"Don't worry about it," Morea murmured. "You can always tell my father we spent a little longer at the lovers' lane than you intended." She reached for the check the waitress had left and watched in astonishment as Ridge slid it out from under her fingertips as smoothly as if he were performing a magic trick. "That ought to be mine," she said firmly. "After all, you are doing me a favor...of sorts."

"Oh, please let me," Ridge said earnestly. "I'll be so much more convincing if I can bury myself in the role."

He dropped a bill on the table and took her arm. "You know, snookums, I like your hair down around your shoulders that way. It makes you look softer somehow. More vulnerable."

Snookums? She had to grit her teeth for an instant before she could smile. "I'll remember to wear it that way if the Madisons end up in court."

Ridge grinned. "Oh, I didn't say I'd fall for the trick. I just might have to close my eyes before I go for the jugular."

Outside Maxie's, Morea turned automatically toward her BMW, but Ridge stood his ground, his hand firm on her elbow. "We'll take the convertible, and I'll bring you back after dinner to pick up your car."

"Why not take mine?"

Ridge shook his head sadly. "What would your father think of you chauffeuring me around?"

Morea cast a jaundiced look at the convertible. "Probably that I showed good sense in not riding in this bucket of bolts." By then, however, Ridge had jiggled the key in the passenger door till the lock gave way and opened the door for her, so she gave up and got in. "Why do you own a car like this, anyway?" she asked as he slid behind the wheel and pushed the button which automatically lowered the convertible's top.

"I took it in trade for some legal work."

She started to laugh. "Does the magnificence of the fee reflect the size of the case or the quality of the advice?"

"Both, actually. This car is going to be a classic, you know—as soon as I have the time to work on it."

"I won't even ask when you expect that will be."

His grin was rueful. "Sometime in the next decade, if I'm lucky."

"That's my whole point, you know. You're always

busy, Ridge. You can't be the starving attorney you'd like me to think you are.''

He stared at her, wide-eyed. "I can't?"

But his startled tone was obviously feigned, and Morea laughed. "I just hope you have a better answer than that for my father when he starts inquiring into your finances." She settled back and started humming a little tune.

The soft summer air was pleasantly warm, but the motion of the car created currents which tugged at Morea's hair. She slid farther down into the passenger seat to protect herself from the wind. The low-slung seat was surprisingly comfortable, cradling her gently.

"Want me to stop and put the top up?" Ridge asked.

"No—I'm already windblown, and we're almost there. Turn left at the next corner."

The block was full of activity—one neighbor was washing a car, another was playing catch with a couple of kids, and the scent of a barbecue drifted across the street. But the Landon house was quiet. "The back door, I think," Morea said. "Unless you insist on formality?"

"Me?" He sounded offended. "And ruin my image?"

"That's what I thought."

Ridge brought the convertible to a halt in the driveway and looked up at the house. Morea followed his gaze, feeling as if she was seeing the place for the first time in years.

The house was on the small side, and it was sturdy rather than stylish. Every brick in the whole structure looked as if it had been scrubbed. The window glass gleamed, and the sidewalk appeared to have been recently swept. The only random, uncontrolled note in the entire scene was the profusion of flowers in each window box.

"You grew up here," Ridge said. It was not a question.

"You expected a mansion?" She reached for the door handle and found it missing. "Excuse me, but how am I supposed to get out of here?"

"Wait for me to come around and help you." He scooped up the sheaf of flowers from the back seat and walked around to open her door. "I'm sure your parents will be impressed that I can make the rampant feminist act like a lady."

Morea didn't bother to answer. Through the glass panel in the back door, she could see Meredith, wrapped in a gaily-printed apron, tossing a salad at the kitchen island. Charles was nowhere in sight, but Morea took a deep breath before she turned the knob and willed enthusiasm into her voice, just in case her father was nearby. "Mom? We're here."

The lines of stress in Meredith's face had eased somewhat since the weekend, and the way she smiled at Ridge as she came to greet him made her look almost like her old self.

That alone was worth the effort, Morea told herself. No matter what ultimately happened, at least Meredith would know she'd done all she could. And if Morea could ease her mother's burden, she was willing to go to any lengths.

Well, she thought, *almost any lengths.*

"Hello, Ridge," Meredith said, holding both hands out to him. "I'm so glad you could come."

"Where's Daddy?" Morea asked.

"Up in his study." A shadow appeared in Meredith's eyes. "He says he's working on his book, but I'm afraid he's only brooding about everything."

"Well, I'm sorry about that," Morea said briskly, "but happy for the chance to talk to you for a minute.

We're going to have to scale back a bit. This idea of inserting Ridge into the family as a prospective member is—"

Ridge interrupted. "One of the more brilliant I've heard lately." He handed Meredith the flowers. "Now I see where Morea gets her legal intuition."

The glare Morea shot at him should have fried him on the spot, but Ridge merely looked at her blandly, his eyebrows lifted slightly.

Meredith raised the sheaf of flowers to her nose. "How lovely these are," she said. "And how thoughtful of you, Ridge. I think you're the first of Morea's friends to think of bringing me flowers."

Ridge's grin was triumphant.

"Morea, darling, there's a crystal vase in the top cabinet. Would you arrange these for me, please?" She smiled at Ridge. "She's very talented with flowers."

"Mother, honestly—"

Ridge interrupted. "Does she always get so embarrassed when someone compliments her?" he asked Meredith in a confidential tone.

Morea growled under her breath and opened the cabinet door, but it was Ridge who reached over her head and took down the vase. He watched with every appearance of fascination as she began trimming and arranging the flowers. Soon he began untangling the stems, handing each flower to her in turn.

Meredith finished the salad and took a platter of cold grilled chicken from the refrigerator.

Morea tried to ignore Ridge, standing close beside her. "That looks wonderful, Mom. Far better than the sort of thing I've been eating on the run lately."

"I thought as warm as it is, a light supper would be more to everyone's taste," Meredith said. "By the way, Charles asked me how you two happened to discover each other. I didn't quite know what to tell him, so I just said—''

Morea's heart sank. She didn't even want to hear what sort of story her mother had spun; at the rate Meredith was going, she'd be eligible for the best-seller list by the end of the year.

''That you met on a case, of course, but all you'd told me is that it was quite a story,'' Meredith finished. ''I thought I should warn you, though, that he's likely to ask for the details.''

''Mother…'' *Thinking on your feet is supposed to be your strong point*, Morea reminded herself. *So prove it—right now!*

''It was the garlic,'' Ridge murmured.

Meredith looked puzzled. ''What did you say?''

Morea tried to fight the blush which rose in her cheeks.

Ridge didn't miss it, of course. ''We were trying in vain to negotiate a property settlement when Morea decided she wasn't getting enough of my attention, so—''

''As if I wanted your attention!''

Ridge picked up a lily and stroked Morea's nose with the soft tip of a petal. ''Now is that any way to convince your father?'' he asked gently.

Morea lowered her voice, but she persisted. ''I figured if I reeked of garlic you'd be anxious to make a deal so you could escape.''

''Exactly. But you didn't know then that garlic is one of my all-time favorite scents—''

''I know what you *said*,'' Morea muttered. ''Which was that you liked my new perfume. And I don't believe it any more now than I did then.''

Ridge turned to Meredith, who was looking back and forth between them as if she were trying to follow the action in a Ping-Pong game. ''I fell in love with her because of it," he said earnestly. Then he frowned. "Do you think that's good enough to convince Charles? Always assuming that Morea learns to cooperate, of course."

Morea made a face at him.

Meredith shook her head, more in confusion than disagreement. "Morea, please go upstairs and tell your father you're here."

Obediently—and also, she had to admit, relieved to be out of Ridge's sphere for a few moments—Morea climbed the stairs. The squeak in the third step from the top was louder than she remembered, and as if it was a summons, it called forth a voice from the nearest room. "That you, Meredith?"

"Sorry to disappoint you, Daddy—it's only me." Morea paused in the doorway of the bedroom Charles Landon had long ago converted into a study. Every wall was lined with bookshelves, all crammed to the bursting point. Even the windowsill was a foot deep in volumes. On the desk next to Charles' computer keyboard was a shorter stack of books, each one sprouting page markers. The top one lay open.

The white-haired man at the desk turned to peer at her over half-framed eyeglasses. "Is it that time already? I'd lost myself in work."

Beyond him, the computer screen blinked lazily. It was blank except for a highlighted heading which said *Chapter One*.

In almost the same instant as Morea's gaze fell on the screen, Charles moved to close the file. His haste, as much as the telltale couple of words, told her that Meredith had been right once more. He hadn't been working on the book; his thoughts had been somewhere else altogether.

Charles got up, moving a little stiffly—as if he'd been

sitting still for far too long. "And don't be impudent, little girl," he said, and held out his arms. "What do you mean, it's only you?"

Morea hugged him close. He was thinner than he'd been just a couple of weeks ago, when she'd seen him last. And was it her imagination, or was there a brittle feel to his body that hadn't been there before? There was no doubt about the way his face had aged...

Her throat threatened to close up. Intellectually, she'd known since the moment her mother confided in her how awful this accusation would be for him. But only now did she admit in her heart that if it wasn't solved—and soon—not only Charles Landon's career would be in danger, but his health and perhaps even his life, as well.

But at the moment—since she'd given Meredith her word—Morea couldn't even admit to knowing about the trouble. All she could do was hug him close and try not to give herself away by bursting into tears.

Charles held her for a long moment, patting her back, and then said, "What's the matter, Morea? Feeling a little sentimental, are you? Well, you should—threatening to put another man at the top of your list, in my place."

"Daddy, no other man can ever fill your shoes."

"Well, I hope he's at least worthy of making the effort," Charles grumbled. "Your mother seems to like him, though. That's a couple of points in his favor."

Morea was startled. So Meredith had admitted to Charles that she'd already met Ridge? *Perhaps it's silly of me*, Morea thought, *but I wish she'd filled me in on all the details!* Exactly where and when had they supposedly met? And why? And, in Meredith's version, had Morea herself even been present?

She opted for the middle ground. "They do seem to hit it off well," she admitted cautiously. That could apply as easily to the chat in the kitchen a few minutes ago as to some unknown past encounter.

"But then, how much can you tell from a few minutes' conversation in a parking garage?"

It was some relief to know that Meredith must have simply edited her errand last week to include running into Ridge, too. "It's much easier to get to know someone over dinner," Morea agreed, and led the way downstairs.

Ridge had moved into the living room and was looking over the family photographs arranged atop the baby grand piano. The two men eyed each other as Morea introduced them, and she tried not to hold her breath. She was more nervous about this meeting, she reflected, than she'd have been if the excuse was real and she was bringing home the man she intended to marry.

The contrast between them was striking. It wasn't a matter of age or hair color which stood out, however. Ridge seemed to ooze energy, while Charles... Charles, she thought, looked like a pastel sketch next to a bold oil canvas.

Ridge was the first to put out his hand. "Hello, sir. Morea tells me your field is English literature, with a special interest in Shakespeare."

Morea blinked. She hadn't told him anything of the sort; Meredith must have.

"My undergraduate degree was in English lit," Ridge went on.

Charles grunted, as if reserving judgment.

Ridge wasn't deterred. "In fact, I'd love to hear what you think about the controversy on the authorship question."

Now that, Morea thought, was a master stroke. She'd underestimated him once more. All Ridge had to do now was keep nodding, and by the time Charles had exhausted the subject of who really wrote the plays of William Shakespeare, he'd think of the young man as the best of buddies. Behind her father's back she gave Ridge a thumbs-up.

"Nonsense," Charles was saying as she retreated quietly to the kitchen to help her mother. "All of it's nonsense. Let me tell you the facts, my boy..."

Meredith was arranging thin slices of peach and kiwi in a delicate tart shell. "He's such a nice young man," she murmured.

"Don't take him at face value, Mother."

"Oh, I know this isn't serious. But sometimes I wonder, Morea, if you aren't missing out by being so devoted to your job. And it's such a difficult job—dealing with families in stress."

"Someone has to do it."

"Yes," Meredith said slowly. "I suppose so. But doesn't it give you a pessimistic view of life and marriage, when you never see the happy ones? I'd so like to see you settled, Morea."

Morea tried to joke the subject away. "If you're going to start in on me about wanting grandchildren, Mom—"

A flicker of concern in Meredith's eyes warned her of movement from the direction of the living room, and Morea added smoothly, "Just give us a little time, all right?"

If it hadn't been for Meredith's warning, Morea would still have sensed Ridge coming up behind her. Only intuition would have warned her, however; for she certainly didn't hear him. In fact, she had no idea how he managed to move so quietly. Despite her best efforts at staying calm, however, she flinched just a trifle when he slid an arm around her waist and drew her back against his chest.

"Right," he said. "As a matter of fact, we haven't

gotten around to discussing the part of the prenuptial contract which concerns children, so at the moment we really aren't able to say whether there will be any at all.''

Meredith laughed.

''Don't encourage him,'' Morea said under her breath.

It was too late, however. Ridge went on, blithely, ''I think we'd better stop at three or four, myself. Braces and private schools and riding and dancing lessons are so expensive.''

''Perhaps,'' Charles said, ''you could negotiate a group rate.''

Ridge looked delighted. ''Now that's a thought. If we were to have a dozen—''

Morea had listened long enough. ''I thought you two were absorbed in the question of Shakespeare,'' she said firmly.

Charles snorted. ''We were. Your young man is dead wrong, of course.''

Morea was horrified. All Ridge had had to do was agree, and he'd have been halfway toward winning Charles' confidence. She twisted halfway around to glare at him; Ridge's arms tightened warningly.

''But at least he's logical about it,'' Charles went on almost grandly, and slapped Ridge on the back. ''Meredith, what's for dinner? A good argument always makes me hungry.''

Ridge's breath tickled Morea's ear. ''Didn't trust me to handle this, did you?''

She didn't bother to answer. Whatever she said, it would only feed his ego—which obviously needed no help at all.

Over the salad and chicken, Charles asked about Ridge's law practice. ''You're not in Morea's partnership, I understand?''

Morea was fairly sure that Ridge, once forewarned, could take care of himself, so she settled back in comfort to observe the cross-examination.

"No, sir," Ridge said politely.

"How about your own practice? Is it successful?"

"Oh, I think so." Ridge's gaze drifted across to meet Morea's. "At least I heard it said once that a law firm is considered to be flourishing if the clients outnumber the partners, so by that standard—"

Morea choked on a bite of cherry tomato.

Ridge looked solicitously across the table at her. "Are you all right, honey?"

"By that standard," she managed, "you're a phenomenal success." Her voice was hoarse. "Not to say a raving genius. An incredible—" Too late, she realized how fascinated her father appeared, and she sobered abruptly. "What I meant, Daddy, is that Ridge's practice is very...exclusive."

Ridge's eyes sparkled with appreciation. "What she's trying to say is that there's only me right now," he said modestly. "I'm hoping, of course, that Morea will leave TBC to join me—but of course I'll understand if she doesn't think she can stand the pressure."

Morea was speechless. She had to grant him credit, and she told him so as soon as dinner was over and they were safely out the door. "That comment of yours had more barbs per syllable than any loaded question I've ever heard before," she accused the moment the convertible was out of the Landons' driveway. "You know perfectly well I wouldn't consider leaving TBC under any circumstances, and implying that I might stay only because I'm afraid of the pressure of solo practice is the single most insulting accusation I've ever had to absorb. Not that it surprises me, coming from you, but—"

"Just one more thing to negotiate in our prenuptials,

I guess," Ridge murmured. "Who has to turn down the case when the opposing sides want to hire both of us."

Morea's irritation vanished in a sudden fit of humor. "Can you imagine seriously trying to work this out? I mean, if a client presented me with this mess..."

"Considering the way TBC has taught you to think, you'd probably have to turn it over to an expert."

"An expert in messes," Morea mused, and smiled. "Come to think of it, Ridge, that's a no-brainer. I'd just call you."

CHAPTER FOUR

MOREA was watching him as she said it. She expected him to laugh off the remark; something so casual couldn't possibly break through armor as well-developed as Ridge's. Still, she was startled by the effect her words seemed to have on him. He was positively aglow with good humor, as if the sun had found itself lost inside him and was trying to seep out. The phenomenon left Morea feeling light-headed and slightly dizzy.

"See?" Ridge pointed out. "That's exactly why I think we'd make great partners."

She shook her head a little, trying to clear it. "If I ever need a job I'll be in touch. But don't hold your breath."

"I never do when I'm waiting for you to reach a conclusion."

"That's a pity," Morea mused. "Because if you held it long enough—"

"Don't pretend you wouldn't miss me, Morea. I wouldn't believe you."

"Of course I'd miss you—just like I miss a bad case of hiccups once it's gone." She sobered. "What do you think, Ridge? About Daddy, I mean."

"I can hardly draw any conclusions when I haven't even heard his description of the situation."

He was right, of course. She'd have said much the same thing herself if a client had asked her opinion. Still, she was almost disappointed that Ridge hadn't figuratively patted her on the head and assured her it would be all right. It was funny, she thought—and a little frightening, too—how quickly her own legal training and professional detachment seemed to vanish when the situation concerned someone she cared for so deeply.

"So much for your steak dinner," she said.

"Oh, I didn't say I'd given up on that. We didn't put a time limit on the deal, you know."

"If it comes to that, we didn't exactly make a deal. I was only saying—"

"Don't try to weasel out of it now, Morea. You know perfectly well you don't have to shake hands on an agreement, much less write it down, in order to have a contract—and it certainly sounded just now as if you'd agreed."

"I hate it when you start treating me like a freshman law student, Ridge."

"Then stop acting like one. I've got just the place in mind, too, for when I win that bet—they serve a beef tenderloin that's the size of a roast, and I plan to enjoy every single bite."

"So how are you planning to get Daddy to confide in you?" He didn't answer right away, and Morea went on warily, "If you're expecting me to take you home to dinner every night till you wear him down—"

"Oh, no. I doubt you could stand the strain. If you really want to be useful, you could nose around the campus and find out everything you can about that student. I assume your mother knows her name?"

"I suppose so. I don't remember if she told me."

Maxie's Bar was doing a booming business with the late-dining crowd, and there wasn't a parking spot to be found within blocks. Ridge stopped the convertible in the traffic lane right next to Morea's BMW and walked around the car to open her door.

"Ridge," she said, "what *are* you plotting?"

"I'm double-parked," he pointed out. "And you're

standing in the middle of the street. It's hardly the time
for a discussion of tactics.''

"And if you weren't blocking traffic, you'd find another excuse not to tell me." Morea groped in her handbag for her car keys.

He smiled. "Of course. You know what they say
about always maintaining a little mystery in your relationship, because it keeps the romance alive. See you
Friday, love—or maybe even before that.''

"I'll try to control my excitement over the possibility," Morea said dryly.

But Ridge only laughed.

Morea was working on Susan Petrovsky's case on
Wednesday morning, preparing for her court appearance
the next day, when her secretary tapped on her office
door and came in. "Sorry to bother you," Cindy said.
"But Mr. Davis is here with a client. He says he talked
to you about the case a couple of days ago.''

Morea had been so absorbed in constructing her argument that for a moment she couldn't even remember
talking to Alan Davis, much less discussing a client. She
frowned for a moment before things clicked into place.
Of course; she'd had other things on her mind in the
executive dining room Monday—namely, finding a good
attorney to take on her father's problems. No wonder
she'd put Alan, and his client who wanted a divorce, out
of her mind.

She glanced at her wristwatch. "So here they are
without an appointment. Or did I miss something on my
schedule?''

"No appointment," Cindy said. "That's why I came
in instead of just buzzing you. He did apologize for the
short notice, though.''

"Alan, or the client?" Morea didn't wait for an answer. She seemed to remember telling Alan something about the sooner she saw his client the better; perhaps that was why he hadn't extended her the courtesy of a warning. "Tell them I can spare half an hour, and bring them in."

She used the few moments until Cindy ushered the pair into the office to wrap up her notes and bundle the pages back into the Petrovsky file. She was just laying it aside when the men came in, and she stood up to extend her hand, taking the opportunity to size up her new client.

He reminded her of Napoleon—short and a little stocky, with a broad chest and a way of carrying himself that made him look larger than he was. His posture also left the impression that he thought very well of himself; Morea half-expected that instead of shaking her hand he'd stick his fingers between his buttons in the manner of the Emperor's portraits. He'd have looked pretty silly if he had, though, she thought, since he hadn't bothered with a coat. His dark hair was so unruly it almost had to have been messed up on purpose, and his gaze was lazy and heavy-lidded.

Bedroom eyes, she thought. *Or at least he thinks they are.*

Alan looked even paler and more washed-out than usual, next to his client, as he made the introductions. "Morea Landon, Trent Paxton. You know the name, of course, Morea?"

She doubted there was anyone in Denver who wouldn't recognize it. The Paxtons had been among Colorado's first settlers, but Trent hadn't gone into the family business. Instead, he seemed to prefer living off his inheritance and dabbling in the entertainment industry.

Alan saw the recognition in her eyes, and nodded.

"Trent's a talent promoter," he said. "The firm has dealt with a number of matters for him over the last few years."

Morea seemed to remember that one of those matters had been defending a suit brought by one of Trent Paxton's clients for nonpayment of royalties on a recording contract. She didn't recall how it had turned out—though she assumed Trent must have been contented with the results or he'd have found another law firm by now. And of course, no matter what the facts of that case, it had nothing to do with his divorce.

"I won't interfere in your conference, Morea," Alan went on, "but I told Trent that he could have complete confidence in you."

Without waiting to be invited, Trent Paxton tossed himself into the chair across from Morea's desk. "Having a woman on my side might not be a bad idea," he conceded. "When you tell the judge that my wife doesn't deserve a cent, he'll sit up and take notice."

"You know we've already talked about that, Trent," Alan said. "It's doubtful that you can get out of this for free, but Morea will do her best to assure that it doesn't cost you—"

"Thanks, Alan," she interrupted crisply. "I think Mr. Paxton and I can take it from here."

He looked at her doubtfully, but without another word he followed Cindy out of the office.

"I don't expect *you'll* be free, of course," Trent Paxton said expansively. "I'll no doubt pay plenty for your services. One thing this firm certainly knows about is sending bills. But I want it understood up front that I don't plan to get stuck for a penny of alimony, and as for this nonsense about her getting a share of the things I own—"

Morea let him talk for a while, but when after ten

minutes he showed no signs of running down, she cut across the stream of invective. "Mr. Paxton, you've used the first third of our conference to tell me how to do my job. Now let me give you a few facts of life."

He looked startled, but he shut up.

"If you pursue your desire for a divorce," Morea said, "one of two things is going to happen. Either you and your wife will come to a mutual agreement on a settlement both of you find reasonable and fair, or the court will create a settlement for you. In either case, since you've been married for several years and have a child, you won't walk away without considerable cost. Not only do you have a responsibility to support your son, but—"

"Whose side are you on, anyway?" he accused. "It certainly doesn't sound like mine!"

Morea went on as if he hadn't interrupted. "Your best move is to try to reach an agreement with your wife so you have some control over what that settlement will be. The more reasonable you are in the beginning, the more likely it is that you'll be able to live with the results. Alienate her, and you may end up with the court dictating a judgment you really hate."

"Whew," Trent Paxton said. "You're one gutsy lady. You know, I don't like you at all."

"Most people hate their divorce attorneys by the time the case is over. Perhaps you've just skipped the first few stages." Morea toyed with a pen. "However, you might want to consider hiring a different attorney. This could be a long and involved process, and you'd no doubt be more comfortable with a representative you trust and respect more than you apparently do me."

He sat as if he'd taken root. "Are you turning me down?"

I'd like to, Morea thought. But refusing to work with

the firm's existing clients was something the senior partners would never forget. Besides, she couldn't see herself going back to Alan Davis and telling him, on the basis of one short interview, that his client was impossible. After all, the only things she really knew about Trent Paxton right now were that he bore a huge resentment against his wife and he'd made a bad impression on Morea herself. The first observation wasn't an appropriate excuse to turn down the case; most men entering the divorce process felt the same. And the second black mark was pure instinct—hardly something she wanted to explain to her legal-minded superiors.

Maybe Ridge had a point after all about the advantages of an independent practice, she mused. He could toss Trent Paxton out of his office—figuratively speaking, at least—and not have to explain to anyone that he'd taken a sudden dislike to the man...

Of course, that brought up another interesting question. *Would* Ridge have disliked this guy? Would he have thrown him out of his office or taken the case and savored the challenge?

She didn't realize she hadn't answered Trent Paxton's question till he spoke again. "Well, are you? Because I want you on this case."

She was startled, and she must have showed it.

"I like the idea that you don't take any guff, even from me." He grinned. "And my wife will like that, too. She'll figure, with the way you talk to me, that you're really on her side. You'll have her eating out of your hand, Morea."

Morea eyed him icily. "It's Ms. Landon, please."

"Whatever you say." He grinned as if he thought she was making a joke. "Daisy will love that bit. So it's a deal, right?"

"We'll give it a try," Morea said warily. "Let's start

by getting the details about the marriage." She looked around her desk, but the usually-efficient Cindy, with no warning, hadn't brought in a packet of blank forms. Morea picked up the phone and asked for them.

A couple of minutes later when Cindy came in, there was a note stuck to the top of the folder where Trent Paxton couldn't see it. *Synnamon Welles wonders if you can have lunch*, Cindy had written.

Morea considered, and nodded. She could benefit from a break to clear her head of the Paxton matter before she tried to go back to the Petrovsky file.

Fifteen minutes later, she had a fair picture of the disheveled state of Trent Paxton's marriage, and a conviction that this case would be more like a war than a divorce. Trent, however, seemed to be perfectly cheerful; even the browbeating Morea had had to do to keep him on the subject had seemed only to increase his good humor.

"Yes," he said, as she eased him out of the office with a promise to see him again the next week, "I knew old Alan wouldn't steer me wrong. Daisy is going to adore you so much she probably won't even hire an attorney of her own." With a wink, he was finally gone.

Morea followed him to the outer office and tossed the folder onto Cindy's desk. "That man," she said coolly, "is the personification of slime. Where am I supposed to meet Synnamon?"

"Right here," a gentle voice said behind her.

Morea wheeled around, eyes wide. "I had no idea anyone was around!"

Synnamon Welles put her hands on her hips. Even the sleek cut of her designer dress couldn't conceal the fact that she was extremely pregnant. "I know what you mean," she accused lightly. "You're wondering how, considering my present shape and sheer size, you managed to miss me.''

"It's not that—you look great. It's just that I didn't expect you to be here.''

"I do not look great," Synnamon objected. "I look like an overweight walrus—but thanks for not telling me so. The fact is I was in the neighborhood and needed to put my feet up, so of course I thought of your office, since TBC has the most comfortable furniture in Denver.''

Morea shrugged. "We aim to serve.''

At an easy pace, they strolled the two blocks to the Pinnacle. Morea's favorite restaurant, it was perched atop one of Denver's premier hotels, with the revolving dining room providing a glorious view of the mountains to the west, the high plains to the east, and the city twenty stories below.

As soon as they were settled at a window table, Morea said bluntly, "I shouldn't have let my mouth run away with me like that.''

Synnamon opened her menu. "I didn't hear a thing, dear.''

"Thanks.''

"Not that I don't agree with you, of course. Trent Paxton is classic pond sludge. The things I've heard his wife say about the way he treats her...''

Morea frowned. "How do you know Daisy Paxton? I don't think I've ever met her.''

"She did some modeling for us a couple of years ago, when we introduced our new no-smudge lipstick. I expect modeling is how she met Trent—at least he was managing her career when we hired her. Why are you hanging around with him, anyway?''

"I'm not.''

Synnamon nodded wisely. "That must mean he's a

client. And since I doubt very much he and Daisy are adopting a baby, it probably indicates a divorce in the works.''

"You shouldn't be speculating, Synnamon."

"Why on earth not? You're the one who took the oath of legal ethics, not me."

"And that same code of ethics means I shouldn't be letting you speculate, either. You don't have a clue how much trouble I could get in."

"Darling, trust me. I won't breathe a word. It's just that as a recent sort-of divorced person myself, I'm fascinated with the ins and outs of—''

"You have far too much time on your hands, Welles."

Synnamon sighed. "That, too. I can't seem to concentrate on anything these days."

"Even your new job?"

"Especially my new job. Besides, every time I try to lift so much as a sheet of paper, Conner's right there fussing at me not to hurt myself. Maybe after the baby's born..." She ran a hand over her abdomen. "I wonder what the kid would like for lunch—or more to the point, what he'll let me eat without giving me heartburn. Two more weeks—tops—and I can go back to ordering for my own tastes. I can't wait." She opened the menu once more. "Why are you representing Trent Paxton, anyway, Morea? If you don't like the man—''

"I don't have to like every client, but I'll still do my best for each one."

"Well, yes, of course. But does that mean you have to take on everybody who asks? That's not a part of the ethics code, is it?"

"No—I can turn down anyone if I don't think I can effectively represent him."

"Well, that excuse covers a lot of territory. You can

let the marsh scum fend for himself without even having to tell him what you think of him."

"The trouble is…" Morea reconsidered, and started over. "Whether I approve of a client or not is hardly the point. Even a serial murderer is entitled to the best representation available, you know." She glanced at her menu and ordered the broccoli quiche.

"Come to think of it," Synnamon mused, "serial murder is just about the only sin Daisy Paxton's never accused Trent of committing." She asked for a chef's salad and handed her menu to the waiter.

The maître d' sidled up to the table. "You have a telephone call, Ms. Landon. Would you prefer to take it here or in the office?"

It was odd that Cindy hadn't just paged her, Morea thought. Perhaps the battery in the pager she always carried had gone dead again; she'd have to remember to check it out. "Here, please."

Synnamon settled back to sip her club soda. "You were saying something about trouble?"

"Don't you ever miss anything, Welles?"

"No. It comes from hanging around with my attorney. You don't mean you're going to take his case anyway?"

"I don't have a lot of choice. He's already a client of the firm, so it would be a little difficult to explain to the senior partners why I don't want to work with him."

"Ah," Synnamon said wisely. "Job security. Having to please the boss is a pain in the neck, isn't it?"

"Well, don't fret—I'm hardly on the thin edge of losing my job even if I turn down a case. And there are a lot more advantages to a big group practice than there are disadvantages."

Synnamon's eyebrows raised slightly. "Gracious, you're touchy. I was only trying to sympathize, not jolt a nerve."

Morea had to admit it was true; she was being sensitive. What she didn't understand was why she sounded so defensive. She did appreciate the advantages of the large practice. She liked being able to call on her partners whenever she needed an opinion or a backup. And she loved being able to specialize in one area of law instead of scrambling to keep up with several as she'd probably have to do in order to make a living as a single practitioner.

But maybe there was a middle ground. *We'd make a great team*, Ridge had said…

And why was she suddenly thinking about him again? she asked herself in annoyance. The fact that Trent Paxton was shaping up to be the Client from Hell didn't mean she was ready to toss aside the career she'd worked so hard to build.

The maître d' returned with a telephone and plugged the cord into a nearby jack. Morea picked it up.

It was as if Ridge had heard her thinking about him and homed in on the signal. "Hello, love," he said comfortably. "Are you having a nice lunch? And do you have any idea how much trouble I had finding you?"

"Obviously not enough," Morea murmured. "Because you succeeded."

"I'm quite proud of myself, too. Haven't you told your secretary yet about our new relationship?"

"It's not a relationship, Ridge."

"Morea, your father would be so disappointed to hear that. I played tennis with him this morning, by the way."

"Congratulations."

"Thanks for your faith in me, dearest—but I lost. It wasn't a strategic loss, either. He beat me fair and square. We had the nicest chat, though."

"Does that mean you're going to try to collect a steak dinner from me?"

"Unfortunately, we haven't worked up to that sort of chat. Mostly we talked about you. When you were a child, were you really as cute as your father seems to think you were?"

"Is there a point to this conversation, Coltrain? Because I'm a little busy just now."

"At least you get to go out for lunch," he pointed out. "I'm still at my desk, trying to make up for the time I lost this morning. Actually, I'm calling to ask you to tea on Sunday."

"Ridge, there's nothing in the world I want to do less than go to tea with you on—"

"It's not just me. And that's not all. Since I've invited your parents, too, and the occasion is to meet my mother, I thought perhaps you'd like to meet her first."

"Your mother," Morea said slowly. "Mrs. Coltrain."

"That's usually what she answers to, yes. I've always thought it's a nice little custom, a married woman taking her husband's—"

"You live with your mother?"

"Well, if you want to be absolutely technical, she lives with me. But if you mean, is she the one you talked to the day you called—"

"I knew it. You never have acted married."

"I could have both a wife and a mother, you know," Ridge pointed out. "It's been done before."

"Not by you."

"Well, now that you mention it, no. If you're free tonight, I'll take you by to meet her."

"I've got a court appearance in the morning."

"I promise not to keep you up all night." The words were innocuous, but there was a sultry note in his voice which made Morea want to hit him. She did the next best thing and hung up on him instead.

Synnamon was looking very thoughtful. "Sorry," she

said. "I'm generally very good at pretending that I didn't hear a word of conversations like that. But if you expect I'm not going to ask what the heck is going on between you and Ridge Coltrain—"

"The usual stuff. A case here, a case there." Morea waved the maître d' down and handed him the phone. "If the gentleman calls back, would you tell him, please, that I just left?"

"Gentleman?" Synnamon said. "I seem to remember that the last time you mentioned Ridge Coltrain to me, you were drinking tomato juice and wishing it was his blood."

"Oh, that was the Simmons case," Morea said airily. "His client got custody, and I thought mine should have. It happens all the time—no big deal."

Synnamon looked a little doubtful. "It didn't sound like it was *no big deal* at the time. And now you're calling him a gentleman? What on earth changed your mind?"

"It's a term of professional courtesy. Doesn't mean a thing." Morea stabbed at her quiche. "Would you like to do me a favor, Synnamon?"

"If you want me to investigate whether he's really married after all—"

"Why would I care?" But Morea had to admit there was a tiny twinge of relief deep inside her. *At least,* she thought, *the fact that he's single limits how seriously this affair can blow up in my face!*

"No? Well, if the favor is not to ask any more questions, I really don't think I could bear to—"

Morea interrupted. "You've got major connections at my father's university, don't you?"

"They seem to remember my name anytime there's a fund-raiser," Synnamon said. She sounded very cautious.

"There's a student of my father's that I'd like to know a whole lot more about."

"Like what?"

"Her academic history, where she came from, what her family's like..." Morea shrugged. "That's part of the difficulty, really. I don't know what's important. I mean, I'll recognize the valuable stuff when I hear it, but I can't go searching myself. The minute my name comes into it, I won't be able to find out a thing."

"I'm afraid I won't be very subtle if it comes to shadowing her. I'm hardly in any condition to be a sleuth." Synnamon shrugged. "But why not? I haven't anything better to do for the next couple of weeks. Being nosy might be sort of fun." She pushed her salad aside almost untouched.

"Is that all you're eating these days?" Morea's own concerns were forgotten. "You can't keep going on two lettuce leaves and a sliver of ham. And as for the baby—"

"He can lump it—or learn not to give me heartburn."

Morea tried to hide her smile. "It's a boy, then? I thought you didn't want to know."

"I didn't. But Conner did, so the doctor told him. And ever since then, he's been going around with such a smug smile, even though he said he didn't care—"

Morea nodded. "—That it has to be a boy."

"Right. Not that he'll admit it, of course. By the way, he mentioned just the other day that he still hasn't gotten a final bill for your services back in the dark ages when you were my divorce attorney."

"Really? I'll check on it. I'd like to say it's my remarriage gift, but I have a feeling TBC's comptroller wouldn't be amused at the idea."

Which brought Morea's thoughts back to the practice again. Sometimes, she mused, it would be nice to make her own rules. Set her fees with the case and the client in mind instead of TBC's rate card. Even go out seeking the cases she would find challenging....

Damn, she thought. In her three years at Taylor Bradley Cummings, she'd never once questioned the decision she'd made to join the firm. Not until she'd run up against Ridge Coltrain and had to throw in her lot with him for her father's sake.

I hope this mess gets settled soon, she thought. *Because if it doesn't, I won't be sure of anything anymore.*

CHAPTER FIVE

MOREA spent the rest of the day studying the Petrovsky case, and when at last she snapped off the lights in her office, she was bone tired but keyed up. She was looking forward to going home and sinking into a long, hot bubble bath. Then she'd have a light dinner and do her last review of the case, making as certain as she could that nothing which happened in court the next day would surprise her. A good night's sleep, and...

But all those plans were made before she realized Ridge was waiting for her. He'd spread the contents of his briefcase across the low coffee table in her waiting room, and he looked as comfortable there as he did in his own office.

Maybe even more comfortable, Morea thought. At least her chair didn't threaten to upset every time he moved, as his did.

"I'd actually managed to make myself forget all about you," she said.

Ridge looked up with a smile and slowly unfolded himself from the low chair. "My darling," he murmured, "how flattering it is to know that it takes all your effort to put me out of your mind!"

Cindy sniffed.

Morea turned toward her with raised eyebrows, a query in her eyes.

Cindy said, "I'd have warned you he was here, but you did say you didn't want to be disturbed for anything short of a natural disaster."

"And what do you call him?" Morea jerked her head

75

toward Ridge and answered her own question. "An unnatural one, I suppose."

"I told Cindy not to bother you." Ridge's smile at the secretary was a thousand watts of pure charm.

"Great," Morea said. "Now you're trying to give my secretary orders."

"Not at all. I was content simply to wait here, for as long as it took you to notice me. Just to breathe the same air—"

"Coltrain, you sound like a bad love poem."

"I'll work on it. Maybe I can set it to music and hit the pop charts." He slid the folder he'd been working on back in his briefcase and snapped the lock. "Ready?"

"No. Look, Ridge, I told you this afternoon, I have a court date tomorrow."

"I know. That's why I waited patiently out here for you, so you could work. Wasn't it thoughtful of me?"

It was—but she was darned if she'd admit it, for he'd probably store up the acknowledgment to use as a bargaining chip some other time. "And now I'm going home to get a good rest—"

"And think about the case?" Ridge asked helpfully.

"Exactly."

He shook his head. "It's not healthy to go over and over things, Morea. You need a distraction at times like this to help you relax."

"A distraction like meeting your mother? I hardly think that would be relaxing." Morea noted that Cindy's eyes had widened in shock. She wanted to bite her tongue off.

"Since you've never met my mother, how would you know?" Ridge picked up his briefcase. "Thanks for the coffee, Cindy. I'm sure we'll be seeing each other again soon." He took Morea's elbow. "Just a quick visit. I'll have you home in plenty of time to drive yourself nuts rehearsing what you're going to say to the judge—if that's really what you want to do all night.''

Morea didn't bother to answer.

In the elevator on the way down to the parking garage, he announced, "I've been thinking all afternoon."

"Poor thing," Morea cooed. "Do you need an aspirin?"

"Thinking is the hardest work there is. That's why so few people end up doing the majority of it. Have you found out anything yet about the student?"

"I've started some inquiries."

He frowned a little.

"I can hardly go out there and introduce myself to her," Morea said, "and ask what on earth she has against my father. So Synnamon Welles is going to ask some questions."

Thoughtfully, he repeated the name. "Wasn't she involved in another of your celebrated cases?"

"As a matter of fact, yes." Morea's tone was chilly. "And I'm quite pleased that they reconciled instead of going through with the divorce. At any rate, once I know a little more about the student, Synnamon and I are going to create a scholarship for her. Tailor-made just for her, so she'll simply have to apply."

Ridge was still frowning.

"The application, of course, will require answers to in-depth questions—maybe even a life story. By the time I'm finished I'll know what she had for breakfast on her fifth birthday."

"I just hope you know something useful."

"Thanks for your confidence. I happen to think the idea's ingenious."

Ridge didn't answer. He unlocked his convertible and held the door for her.

Morea stood her ground. "Come on, Ridge. I'll even let you drive the BMW."

"No, thanks."

"Don't you want to impress your mother with how successful I am?" she wheedled.

"Hadn't thought about it, no."

Of course not, Morea concluded. Why would his mother care what kind of person she was? The only reason for bothering with this introduction was so they'd all be better able to perform for Charles and Meredith on Sunday. *Tea!* Morea could just about imagine how much fun that was going to be.

"How did I ever get into this mess, anyway?" she grumbled.

Ridge shot a look at her. "Funny. I keep asking myself the same thing."

Morea was startled for a moment. Then she began to smile, and she was feeling positively cheerful as she snuggled down in the low seat of the convertible. She might be dreading a formal Sunday tea with his mother and her parents—tiny sandwiches, dainty cups, upraised pinky fingers and all. But it was obvious that Ridge wasn't looking forward to the occasion, either. And since the whole thing had been his idea, she might even derive some amusement from watching him squirm.

Of course, she realized, there was an alternative explanation for his reaction, too. He had no personal stake in this case as she had, no reason to look forward to the work and time it would involve. And since he knew the limits of Charles and Meredith Landon's finances, Morea wouldn't be surprised if—out of the goodness of his heart—he ended up understating both the number of hours he put in and his normal rate of pay. It was exactly the kind of thing Ridge would do...

She was annoyed at having to grant him any such

virtue, and there was an edge to her voice as she said, "I've already told you I'll be responsible for your bill, Ridge. I don't want my parents even to see it. So make sure you're keeping track of all your time."

For a moment, she thought he hadn't heard. He'd left the convertible's top up today, but the breeze whipped through the open windows, teasing the silky scarf at Morea's throat and roaring in her ears.

"Ridge? I said—"

"Does that include things like dinner and tennis, too?" He sounded only mildly interested.

"Yes, as long as you'd bill the service to any other client under the same circumstances." Her voice was tart.

"But, darling, I've never encountered circumstances like these before. Perhaps you can teach me how a Taylor Bradley Cummings' attorney approaches—"

"And don't worry about how long this is likely to tie you up," Morea went on firmly. "I've already started looking for the best attorney I can find to represent Daddy, once you've convinced him to fight."

The silence dragged out for a long moment. "It drives you crazy to be on the same side of things with me, doesn't it, Morea?"

Morea bit her lip. Though she wasn't exactly sure why, that accusation cut just a little too close to the bone to be comfortable.

"You can't quite decide if you want me to succeed for your father's sake," Ridge mused, "or fall flat just to satisfy your baser instincts. Can you?"

Of course she didn't want him to fail; her father's career depended on it. Knowing Ridge, however, a success would only make him even more obnoxiously self-assured and difficult to deal with. Well, she'd face that when she had to—and count herself lucky, if only her father came out of it all right.

She tried to make light of the accusation. "Frankly, I'd be happy to get through this without committing murder."

"Well, that's good. Because I really couldn't see myself defending you."

"Not if you were the victim, no."

"Exactly," Ridge said easily. "What did you think I meant?"

The convertible eased into a narrow driveway beside a tall old house. "I think I'm seeing things," Morea said warily. "There can't really be a birdcage the size of a three-car garage in your backyard, can there?"

"And you with your expensive education," Ridge chided. "Don't you know an aviary when you see one?" He strolled around the car and paused to greet a silky-haired Irish setter who reared up, paws on Ridge's shoulders, to lick his face. "Mind your manners, Flanagan," he ordered. "We have a guest."

The dog dropped to his haunches, and Ridge opened the car door for Morea.

She didn't move. "Do you raise parakeets in your spare time, or what?"

"In the aviary? Of course not, they'd freeze. That's for the owls and hawks. Occasionally when there aren't any raptors we use it for other birds, but that's a rare—"

"Owls? Hawks?"

"Injured ones," Ridge said patiently. "Or orphaned ones. My mother nurses them back to health, or raises them till they can forage for themselves."

"But isn't it illegal to have birds like that?"

"I certainly hope not. If the stack of licenses and certificates she has isn't enough to keep her on the right side of the law, I don't want to know about it. And by the way, the aviary's only the size of a *two*-car garage. I know, because we tore the old garage down and used the foundation.''

Morea slid out of the car. She almost tripped over the dog, who was sitting patiently on the walk, one paw outstretched in greeting. ''Oh, I'm sorry,'' she told him. ''Flanagan, was it? It's nice to meet you.'' She bent to shake his paw, and the excited dog reared up into her face. Startled, Morea reeled back into Ridge's arms.

His hands rested warmly on her hips, and the off-balance weight of her body pressed her spine against his chest. His warmth seemed to course through her bones, and Morea could smell the subtle mix of cologne and soap clinging to his skin.

''Sorry,'' Ridge said. ''I should have warned you that where obedience training is concerned, Flanagan's memory is a whole lot shorter than his hair.'' He set Morea gently back on her feet, but he didn't let her go.

The dog, looking puzzled, twisted his head to one side and studied her. Cautiously, Morea bent to scratch his ears.

''Keep that up and you'll have a devoted slave,'' Ridge warned. ''Come in and meet my mother.''

Morea had braced herself for almost anything, but the kitchen he took her into was neat and normal, with bright yellow curtains at the big windows and warm wood cabinets lining the walls.

At the island in the center of the kitchen, a tall, rangy woman with a deeply lined face leaned over a basket, an eyedropper in her hand. ''Come on, now,'' she said firmly, and picked up a tiny pink lump from the basket.

Morea edged closer. ''Is that a rabbit?''

''Someday it will be, if it's lucky.'' The woman inserted the eyedropper into the rabbit's tiny mouth and squeezed, then set the animal back in the basket and turned to look at Morea. "So you're the young woman who's occupying what's left of my son's mind."

Morea didn't quite know how to answer that. She glanced at Ridge, and was a bit surprised to see the corner of his mouth tighten. But his voice was as lazy as ever. "Rowena Coltrain—Morea Landon. Where'd the rabbits come from, Mom? They're not your usual thing."

"Down the block. One of the neighbors mowed over the nest. He panicked and snatched the rest out, so now of course the mother wouldn't come back if we begged her."

Morea peered into the basket. "What are their chances?"

"Slim to none," Rowena said. "Just as well, too—if I save them, by next year they'll consume every garden in the neighborhood and I'll be the least popular person around." But even as she spoke, Rowena Coltrain scooped up and fed the other three infants with sure and tender hands. "There," she said. "Pop the appetizers under the broiler, Ridge, and as soon as I wash up, I'll join you on the porch."

Ridge investigated the refrigerator and found a tray of tiny pizza-like snacks. He slid the pan into the oven and reached for Morea's elbow. "I think we've received our marching orders," he murmured. "You've definitely passed muster, by the way. Not just everyone gets invited onto Mother's porch."

The room he led her to was not the screened-in patio Morea had expected from Rowena's description, but a den and sunroom which combined to form the most peaceful—and cluttered—space she'd ever encountered. Books and papers were piled haphazardly on almost every surface, and the long rays of the setting sun spilled across comfortably worn furniture. In the corner a half-finished watercolor sat on a painters' easel, and the window ledge was occupied by the most realistic sculpture of a squirrel that Morea had ever seen.

She sank into a barrel-shaped chair. "Is your mother an artist?" She pointed at the painting.

"Good heavens, no. She considers watercolors therapeutic. I thank my stars she doesn't take it seriously or we'd have that sort of thing all over the house."

Morea bit her lip to keep from smiling. "Well, I wondered if the painting was lacking something or if I was."

"Believe me, it's not you." His tone was firm.

Somehow—though Morea knew he wasn't really declaring her to be perfect—she felt as if she'd received a compliment. It was absolutely foolish, she told herself, but there was a tiny glow deep inside her anyway.

"Would you like a drink?" Ridge rummaged in a small refrigerator which seemed to serve as an end table beside a faded wing-backed chair. "Lemonade? Iced tea? A glass of wine?"

"The lemonade sounds wonderful." Morea let her gaze drift over the room. Funny, she'd have sworn the tail of the squirrel sculpture was fluffed out more than that and held up higher...

In one fluid leap, the sculpture glided from the window ledge to Ridge's shoulder and then to the interior of the refrigerator.

Morea gasped, "It's alive!"

"Not for long, at this rate." Ridge fumbled inside the refrigerator. "When I get my hands on you, you little rodent..." He seized the offending animal by the nape of the neck and held it up at arm's length for a scolding. The squirrel chattered back, sounding irritable, till Ridge set it firmly on the window ledge once more. Then it turned its back on him as if offended.

Morea tried to choke back her laughter, but without

much success. The squirrel was the first living being she'd ever known to give Ridge Coltrain as good as he got—and that made him a hero in Morea's book.

"What's so funny?" Ridge asked. He set a tall cold lemonade beside her.

"Boy, your childhood must have been a barrel of laughs."

"It sure was. Other kids had to settle for stuffed animals and rubber ducks. I always had the real thing. I got a little tired of the swan, though."

"Swan?"

"She'd broken a wing, so she occupied our bathroom till she healed enough to go back to the park. Which meant we had to move her out of the tub every time someone wanted to take a bath."

"Charming," Morea said faintly.

Ridge grinned. "Oh, it had its good side. I'm a champion bathtub-scrubber because of that swan. But that's why the first thing I did when I came back to Denver was to install an extra bathroom and forbid my mother to set foot—or wing or paw—in it."

"Where were you before? And why did you—" She stopped abruptly as Rowena came in with a glass plate piled with snacks, still sizzling. The dog trailed behind her, his nose twitching.

"Has he been too busy flirting to tell you the details?" Rowena said. She set the plate down on an oversize ottoman by Morea's chair. "He was in Phoenix for years. Then I got to feeling a little out of sorts and he came home to make sure I was all right. Bought my house out from under me—"

"Purely in self-defense," Ridge said. "At least that way I have a fighting chance of keeping the furry and feathered tenants out of my bed. And you know perfectly well I was tired of Phoenix, Mom."

Flanagan's nose edged closer and closer to the tray of snacks. Rowena, without looking at him, snapped her fingers, and the dog sank down on his haunches on the faded Oriental rug. "He gave up a thriving practice—"

Ridge offered the snack tray to Morea and munched one himself with evident enjoyment. "What's in this, Mom? It tastes a little different than usual."

Morea hesitated with the tiny pizza two inches from her mouth. The tidbit *looked* all right.

"Don't worry," Rowena told her. "The animals eat all sorts of stuff you don't want to talk about, but there's nothing odd about the human cuisine around here, regardless of what Ridge says."

Morea smiled. She liked Rowena's dry humor and her down-to-earth style. And the porch, though it was shabby, was the most comfortable room she'd seen in years. She relaxed, leaning back into the soft comfort of a chair which seemed to sag in all the right places.

Flanagan gave up on the snacks and flopped on the floor at Morea's feet, in a puddle of sunshine. A moment later the squirrel landed on top of him. The dog reared up, barking, and the squirrel bounded away, landing safely atop a bookcase just out of range, where he preened his tail and looked smug.

No, Morea realized, not *the* squirrel, for the one Ridge had plucked from the refrigerator was still pouting on the window ledge. It was *another* squirrel.

Rowena scolded the dog, who subsided, quivering, onto the floor again, casting worried looks up at the bookcase now and then. "Should I move the animals out for Sunday, do you think? Will your parents be offended?"

If they are, Morea almost said, *it'll be easier to explain to Daddy why this supposed romance isn't going to work out.*

"Usually they're pretty well behaved," Rowena went on, "but once in a while one of the squirrels takes a notion to help himself, and my walnut scones are their very favorite food."

"Except for Christmas fruitcake," Ridge said lazily. "Which doesn't say much for their judgment, of course, but it's a good thing somebody will eat it or the planet would sink under the weight." The squirrel he'd extracted from the refrigerator crept up the winged back of his chair, then launched abruptly onto his shoulder. Ridge didn't even flinch. She watched as he put out a big hand and gently scratched the squirrel's chin as if the animal were a cat.

Rowena looked genuinely worried. "I wouldn't like them to be put off," she began. "It's so important, I think, to make good first impressions in situations like this."

"Don't change a thing," Morea said.

"Really? Do you mean it? I'm sure I'll like your parents, Morea. Anyway, as I was telling you, when I had the little episode with my heart, Ridge—"

"Sorry to interrupt, Mom." Ridge stood up, stretching, with the animal still balanced, its claws entrenched in the fine fabric of his white shirt. "But I promised Morea I'd get her home early since she's got a case tomorrow."

Morea rose and looked around, reluctant to leave the peace and comfort of the shabby little porch. Almost unconsciously, she sighed as she turned to face Ridge.

He was watching her, his gaze sharper than she'd ever seen it before and with an intimacy which instantly brought rich color to her face. For an instant Morea felt like the centerfold of a men's magazine; then she told herself not to be ridiculous. She bore only the sketchiest resemblance to the women in those photographs—and even if she looked like them, she couldn't imagine Ridge staring at her with that kind of interest in his eyes.

Though why the mere idea of him looking at her with desire, instead of his usual cool logic, should make her blush was beyond her understanding.

He moved so quickly that he was almost a blur, and before Morea could react he was beside her, sliding his hand into the pocket of her suit jacket. The sheer unexpectedness of the action, coupled with the sudden warmth of his hand resting against her hipbone, almost robbed her of her voice, and she had to make an effort to speak. "I've run into some guys with roaming hands before, Coltrain—but never one with a pocket fetish."

Ridge extracted his hand, and Morea realized it hadn't been his warmth she'd felt at all, but that of yet another squirrel, this one the tiniest of all, which had slipped unnoticed into her pocket.

He held out the tiny ball of fur, balancing it on his open palm. "I will now accept your apology," he said mildly. "Unless of course you'd rather I just gave the squirrel back. He seems to think you'd make a good mommy."

Morea could feel warmth rushing over her for the third time in less than three minutes. Why was it, she raged, that Ridge Coltrain could make her lose her cool, when she prided herself on her calm, her logic, her unflappability?

"No, thanks," she said stiffly. "And I'm sorry."

"Isn't she gracious?" Ridge murmured. "See you later, Mom. I have a couple more hours' worth of work to do myself." He handed the tiny animal to Rowena.

Flanagan followed them to the car and stood on the sidewalk, head drooping mournfully, until Ridge told him to get in. "Unless you mind?" he asked Morea.

She shook her head, but soon realized why he'd asked.

The setter leaped into the convertible's infinitesimal back seat, but before they were two blocks down the street he'd planted his chin firmly on Morea's shoulder. "Sorry," Ridge said. "But it's a compliment, really. He doesn't do that to people he doesn't like. My mother obviously likes you, too."

"Your mother thinks this is real. Ridge, why haven't you told her we're only pretending to be attracted to each other?"

"Don't tell me you spent an hour with her without figuring out she's not the world's best actress."

"Well, yes. But..." Morea's voice trailed off. Rowena was straightforward, direct—far too candid to take on the sort of role she and Ridge and Meredith were playing. "You could have warned me, at least," she complained.

"Why? I'm confident you can cope with any kind of circumstances."

Morea wasn't so sure that was a compliment. "Then why did you bring Rowena into it at all? It's not as if we're trying to convince Daddy that the wedding is imminent, after all."

"We're not? Then all the work I've done on the prenuptial settlement is in vain?"

"Honestly, Ridge—"

"For instance, I think it's only fair if you take care of paying for the children's braces, if any, since all my family has perfect teeth."

"*You* won't, when I get finished pushing them down your throat."

"Then there's the question of whether you're going to take my name. Socially, at least, life would be so much simpler if every time we introduce each other we don't have to keep two names straight. And think of the children—"

Despite her best efforts, Morea couldn't keep the picture out of her mind. Children—with her own dark hair, Ridge's sunny grin, and the devastating logic that both of them shared...

She shivered. "With us as parents, they'd give an entirely new spin to the subject of sibling fights."

Ridge considered. "You're probably right about that. Professionally, of course, I can understand why you might like to keep your own name. Still, Coltrain & Coltrain would be easier to manage than Coltrain & Landon, and since you'll be making an entirely new start it would be the best time to—"

"It's a good thing you took the handle off this door, Ridge, or I'd be tempted to throw myself out."

"I didn't take it off. It's just missing."

"Whatever. Remind me to get you a new one for Christmas."

"That's very thoughtful of you. But you're changing the subject. Does the threat to do away with yourself mean you don't want to change your name? What a pity. Your father strikes me as a very traditional—"

"You're the one who's changing the subject," Morea pointed out. "If you don't mind having your mother think you're wild about me, why didn't you want her to tell me all about you?"

"You know mothers. Always exaggerating."

She smiled, and said slyly, "Then your practice in Phoenix wasn't a thriving one after all?"

"Of course it thrived," Ridge said with dignity, and then spoiled the effect by grinning. "Mostly because Phoenix is too hot in the summer to do anything except work, but—"

"Will you be serious?" Morea shifted in her seat. "Friday's our settlement conference with Bill and Kathy Madison. I know you said it was your turn to host—but

I think it should be in my office because it's a whole lot more comfortable.''

"Expecting it to take a while, are we?"

Morea shrugged. "Maybe we can get it wrapped up—if you'll be reasonable."

"I'm always reasonable. And in this case, I'm certainly not the one who's holding out for the impossible. That business is Bill's, and he's not wild about giving Kathy a silent partnership, much less anything more than that.''

"Then, if he gets the whole thing, what's he willing to offer her in exchange?"

"Does that mean she'd consider a swap?"

"Depends on what it's worth—but maybe."

"I'll certainly ask him. Suddenly you sound a bit impatient to get rid of this case, Morea."

"Not at the expense of my client," she said firmly. "But I will admit, what with Daddy's troubles and the Husband from Hell, life's getting a bit complicated."

"The Husband from... Is this a new client, darling?"

Morea was already regretting allowing her tongue to run away with her. "I've said all I intend to. I'm certainly not giving you a name so you can call up the unfortunate wife to ask whether she needs an attorney.''

"You just don't want to go up against a pro any more often than you have to, do you?"

"And you don't really want me as a partner, Ridge—you'd much rather keep me as an opponent."

He didn't answer for a moment, and Morea looked at him curiously, wondering what he was thinking.

The office tower loomed up before them, and he threaded the convertible neatly into the parking garage and up the ramp to where Morea had left her car.

"It *is* fun," he mused. "But I wouldn't worry about

it, sweetheart. I'm sure if you decide to be partners I could come up with some other games to take the place of arguing things out in court—ones we'd both like to play.''

I sometimes wish I could believe in reincarnation. I
could catch up with some other games in case I've piled
up enough of them... or in case somehow we'd both like...
him...

CHAPTER SIX

MOREA drove home with only half her mind on traffic,
and as she stepped into the lobby of her condo tower,
she was still wondering exactly how Ridge managed,
time after time, to goad her into saying more than she
meant to. She'd learned to mind her words years ago,
but now that she'd run up against Ridge Coltrain, all of
a sudden she couldn't seem to keep her tongue under
control.

It wasn't even as if Ridge made any real effort to
provoke her; that was what was truly annoying. Or
maybe that was his secret, she thought; he was so ludi-
crously at ease that she let her guard drop, and the next
thing she knew she was off balance again.

Games we'd both like to play— Indeed! The man was
a champion when it came to double entendre. But comments like that meant nothing, really, she told herself.
Ridge just had to get in the last word. He obviously had
no intention of giving up the unholy glee he got from
baiting her—whether in a courtroom or out—for the
questionable pleasure of…whatever he'd meant when
he'd talked of *other games*.

She couldn't help wondering exactly what he'd had
in mind, though. Or, more to the point, what he *would*
have meant if he'd been serious. Which of course he
wasn't, so there was no sense whatever in wondering
what it would be like to kiss—*really* kiss—Ridge
Coltrain.

Besides, Morea told herself, kissing was a nonverbal

sort of game, and Ridge was probably incapable of shutting up long enough for anything of the sort!

When she paused at the main office in the lobby to pick up her mail, the concierge was on the telephone, and she was startled to see her father waiting by the desk. A department store garment bag was draped over his shoulder, and he looked as if he'd been standing there for some time.

"Daddy," she said, "what are you doing here?"

Charles Landon turned to face her. "Hello, Morea. No wonder the concierge wasn't getting an answer from your apartment. I'm not intending to move in, so don't look at me that way."

Wasn't it a trifle odd, Morea thought, that his reaction to such a simple question had been to protest immediately that he *wasn't* leaving home? Was the pressure between him and Meredith even worse than she'd thought?

The knot which had lain in Morea's midsection ever since her mother had first confided in her grew a little larger and twisted painfully tight.

"Your mother found this at her favorite store and thought you might like it," Charles went on. He held out the bag. "It was on sale, she said. She wanted me to drop by so you could try it on."

That wasn't unlike Meredith, who not only had exquisite taste and an eye for a bargain but a lot more time to shop than Morea did. But Morea thought the contents of the bag were probably only an excuse to send Charles over, so Morea could talk to him in private.

"Come on up," she said. "I was just going to scramble an egg for dinner, if you'd like to join me."

Was it only her imagination, or did Charles hesitate? Before Morea could be quite certain, he swung the bag over his shoulder again and followed her to the elevator.

"All right. And I won't even tell your mother how you're eating these days."

Morea smiled at him. "For that, I'll reward you with an extra slice of cheese on top of your serving." She tried not to watch him in the elevator, but it was hard to keep from studying the new lines in his face, the drawn look of his mouth, the way his eyes seemed to have retreated from the world.

How could anyone so much as glance at Charles and not know something was desperately wrong? Especially someone who cared as deeply about him as Morea did. Was Meredith right that he wanted to hide his problem from his daughter, and that Morea would only cause him additional pain if she insisted on answers? Or was she actually adding to the problem by pretending not to see it? Charles might even think Morea found him suddenly insignificant, if she could miss seeing such a change in him—and the last thing he needed just now was that sort of blow to his self-esteem....

You don't know what you're asking, Mother, she thought. *I can't just pretend not to see what's going on. I have to do something...*

Morea waited till her back was turned to her father, as she was inserting her key into the lock, before she spoke. "You look as if you don't feel well, Daddy."

Then she held her breath. Would he tell her, after all?

She could almost feel the tension in his shrug running through her own body. "It's nothing important. I'm just not as young as I used to be, and I don't have the energy I used to have for teaching. I'm thinking of giving it up, in fact." There was a note of bravado in his voice.

Morea hesitated. "Retiring, you mean?" She pushed the door open, and her father followed her into the condo.

Charles didn't answer. "Haven't you done anything with this foyer yet, Morea?"

Morea looked around as if she'd never seen the place before. The previous owner of her condo had wallpapered the foyer in what Meredith called extremely-*faux* marble, and though Morea had always disliked the result, she'd never found the time to do anything about it. In fact, she'd learned to walk through without paying attention at all—which was precisely what she'd always thought Charles did, too. At least, she'd never noticed him showing much interest in interior design before.

But then it would be no surprise if he wanted to change the subject. She, too, would like to pretend this trouble didn't exist.

She led the way through a large and minimally furnished living room to her kitchen, and assumed what she hoped was an innocent-looking frown. "I thought you had another five years till you could even consider retiring."

"Oh, no, it's not that long. And I've got so much sick leave built up it hardly matters, anyway."

He was good, Morea thought with admiration. If she didn't know better, she'd almost believe he was telling the truth. Diplomacy was obviously going to get her nowhere. Did she dare push harder, or actually confront him? If she did, he'd know that Meredith had told her...

While she thought about it, Morea got a basket of eggs out of the refrigerator and her best frying pan from the cupboard.

"Anything I can do to help?" Charles asked.

"You might dig around in the freezer. There should be a package of bagels."

He found them and reached for a knife. "I like this room. It's peaceful."

"Thanks. It's my favorite, too. Daddy—"

Charles went straight on. "A bit unlived in, though. Your mother says this whole place looks more like a hotel suite than a home."

Obviously, Morea thought, Charles aimed to give her no further opportunity to ask uncomfortable questions. Well, she'd bide her time—but that didn't mean she was giving in altogether, just reconsidering her options.

Charles went on, "But I'm sure that'll change when Ridge moves in, won't it?"

Ridge—sharing her home? Her space? Her life? Morea couldn't imagine any such thing.

No, she admitted, the trouble was that she *could* imagine it—and the picture which came to her mind sent shivers up her spine. For one thing, she wondered how peaceful Charles would find her kitchen if he had a couple of baby squirrels watching every move he made. And she could imagine his reaction the first time one of them snatched a scrap of bagel.

Nonsense, she told herself. The squirrels didn't even belong to Ridge. Even if he were to move in...

The shiver intensified. Ridge was hard enough to handle for limited periods of time. She couldn't fathom being constantly exposed to the intensity which lay under his lazy exterior; the very idea was exhausting to consider—and, somehow, a bit exciting, as well.

Charles was studying her with narrowed eyes, and Morea hastily pulled herself back to reality. Contemplating such an idiotic idea was a complete waste of time.

"Ridge has a perfectly good house of his own," she said.

Charles started to frown.

Morea added hastily, "And regardless of what Mother thinks, Ridge and I haven't talked about permanent arrangements, either. Living or otherwise."

"He has a house? I wouldn't have thought..." Charles seemed to catch himself up short. "Not that he doesn't seem solid and reliable, but somehow..."

"He doesn't appear the type? Maybe you should get to know him better. It's hard to talk while you're playing tennis, or with other people around. Why don't I invite him over now," Morea said, trying to keep her voice casual, "and you can have a good chat—just the two of you?"

Charles nodded. "I suppose sooner or later I'll need to ask him whether his intentions toward you are honorable." There was a spark of his old humor in his eyes; Morea didn't realize how long it had been since she'd seen it.

She reached for the telephone, and only then remembered that Ridge had said he was going to his office for a couple of hours—and she didn't have the phone number. "Darn it," she said. "I suppose I'll have to call information again."

"You don't know his number by heart?" Charles joked.

"I've got an automatic dialer at the office. Plug in the number once and you never have to remember it again—but those things absolutely ruin one's memory." That much was factual, she told herself—even if it wasn't the entire truth, by a long shot. "And Ridge just moved into a new office, so the number's not in the book yet."

She held her breath as she dialed. Did he even bother to answer the phone when he worked late? Morea herself never did; the whole point of the evening and weekend hours she spent in her office was to work without interruption. But then Taylor Bradley Cummings paid a small fortune for the most professional answering service available, so there was never a question of losing a message. Would Ridge take the chance of missing a client's call?

"Coltrain," he said in her ear. He sounded preoccupied, but still the low voice caressed her ear the way a satin sheet felt against her skin.

"Ridge—" Mindful of Charles standing only three feet away, she added, "—dear..."

His voice warmed. "Morea, my pumpkin! Do you miss me already? And so much?"

"Terribly. I wondered if you'd like to come over for a while."

"Gracious," Ridge said. "Should I call an ambulance right now, or do I dare wait to see what's wrong with you when I get there?"

"My father's here, and he was just saying that you two really haven't had a chance to get to know each other."

The lazy amusement was gone. "Does that mean you think he's ripe to talk?"

Morea wondered tartly if he actually thought she'd give him a straightforward answer. "I'll expect you here in a few minutes, then."

"I'm on my way. Just one thing, Morea—where's *here*?"

She wanted to groan. She could hardly give him a street address; Charles would be onto that in a split second, questioning why Ridge didn't already know it. And why hadn't Ridge the Omniscient thought of this complication before now?

You ought to have thought of it yourself, she mused. *It's hardly fair to blame it all on Ridge.*

"I'm cooking dinner at the moment," she said sweetly. "Shall I scramble an egg for you?"

"No, thanks—I hate them. But I take it the question means you're at home. I just hope you're listed in the phone book, because I don't keep a copy of the social register on my desk.''

''You're so thoughtful, darling,'' she said, and put the telephone down before he had a chance to create any further complications. ''He said we should go ahead with dinner,'' she improvised, ''because he's already eaten.'' And if he hadn't, she thought, he deserved to go hungry.

Over the simple meal, she asked about the progress of Charles' book, and he inquired about her cases. Afterwards, he volunteered to clear the dishes so she could try on the dress Meredith had sent over. ''Because she said if it doesn't fit she has to take it back tomorrow,'' he said.

Morea glanced surreptitiously at her wristwatch. There should still be time; even if Ridge had left the office the moment she'd hung up, it would take him a while to get to the condo tower. And the concierge would call from downstairs, anyway, to warn her of the visitor.

The garment bag contained not a tailored suit as she'd expected, but a dinner dress of a fabric so soft each fold seemed to float about her body. The way the full skirt draped made Morea feel utterly feminine, and the color was such a brilliant white that the dress actually felt cool against her skin.

It wasn't the kind of thing that Meredith usually chose for her, or that Morea was apt to select for herself. But it felt perfect. The fact that at the moment she had no place to wear it entered her mind, and was promptly dismissed.

She had just come out of her bedroom to model the dress for her father when the doorbell rang. Charles came from the kitchen, a dish towel still wrapped around his waist as a makeshift apron, and met her in the foyer just as she pulled the door open.

Ridge's eyebrows raised as he surveyed the drifting folds of her dress. "I'd suggest you slip into something more comfortable," he murmured, "except that you already look pretty much at ease."

Before Morea could even step back from the door, he'd leaned over to put a soft kiss on her lips. Despite the casualness of the gesture, the warmth of his mouth seemed to linger long after the actual contact was broken. In fact, her lips continued to tingle, and Morea had to fight off the urge to rub them as she might a foot which had gone to sleep.

"How did you get here so quickly?" she asked. "And the concierge—"

"Waved me straight through the lobby."

She felt a silky touch on her ankle and glanced down to see Flanagan pawing at her shoe. His ear had flopped forward and was dragging across the top of her foot. "Dog and all?" she said incredulously.

"Darling." Something just short of a warning crept into Ridge's voice. "You'd think Flanagan and I had never been here before."

Morea swallowed hard. He was dead right; she'd have to be more careful. "Well, don't let me keep you two from your talk."

"Do you think she's trying to get rid of us?" Ridge asked Charles. "I suppose it's just as well, really, if you *don't* hear all the haggling about your dowry, Morea, but—"

Morea sniffed and pointed to the door of the bedroom she'd transformed into an at-home office. Ridge smiled, told the dog to stay, and led Charles down the hall.

Morea hung the new dress in her closet and put on

jeans instead. She was darned if she'd even pretend to dress up for Ridge's sake.

She could hear the low music of masculine voices from her office when she came out, and she avoided the temptation to stop and listen by walking straight past the door.

Flanagan was still where Ridge had left him, precisely in the center of the foyer, sprawled out with his nose pointing hopefully to where he'd last seen his master. Morea had to step over him to get to the living room.

The kitchen was clean; Charles had left nothing to do there. She couldn't even write a check to her mother for the dress, for she kept her household accounts in the office that Ridge and Charles were occupying now. And she couldn't occupy herself with one last review of the Petrovsky file, either; even if her briefcase hadn't been stranded in the office with the men, she wouldn't be able to concentrate just now.

Talking about dowries, indeed, she thought. She only hoped that Ridge's instincts would tell him how to break through Charles' shell. She wondered if he'd try persuasion, sympathy, or confrontation—or something else, something she hadn't even considered.

Well, if anyone could do the trick, it was Ridge. Her mother's gut feelings had been right about that, Morea admitted. She'd never run into anyone who could be quite as compelling as Ridge Coltrain—when he wanted to be. Even while he was beating her into a pulp in the Simmons case, she'd had to admire the strength of his argument. In fact, by the time he'd finished, she'd had to fight off the conviction that he might be right after all.

Funny, she thought. She'd never confessed that even to herself before.

She opened the patio door between living room and

balcony and sat down on the couch. The softness of a summer evening wafted into the room, bringing with it the scent of roses from somewhere far below. The distant twitter of birds seemed to draw Flanagan's attention; he wandered in from the foyer and flopped at her feet.

The painting on the opposite wall, above the gas-log fireplace, was askew. Morea wondered idly how long it had been that way. Since the housekeeping service she'd employed had gone out of business, perhaps. How long was that, now, anyway? A month, perhaps?

She kept forgetting to ask Cindy to look for a replacement. There wasn't much to clean, anyway; one person who spent so little time at home didn't create much of a mess. Only her office was ever cluttered—and she'd never allowed the cleaning service to do anything more than vacuum the rug in that room, anyway.

She wondered if the office had gotten as dusty as the living room had. She wondered if Ridge would notice. Probably not, she decided. Anyone who'd once shared a bathroom with a swan could surely overlook a little thing like a bit of dust.

It felt odd, though, looking around at what should be a familiar place and seeing it through a stranger's eyes. How long had it been since she'd really noticed this room?

Her furniture was a couple of years old now, but even a careful observer wouldn't be able to tell, for there was no wear on the upholstery, not even a crushed cushion on the couch. The tables at each end of the long couch were not only intended to serve that function—unlike the small refrigerator on Rowena's sunporch—but they matched, and the surfaces gleamed. Or at least they did when they weren't covered with a film of dust.

She searched out a soft cloth and an almost-empty can of furniture polish and restored the gleam to the tabletops. The scent of lemon oil stirred a housewifely instinct deep inside her, and she turned her attention to the mantel, the picture frames, the lamp shades. She sorted out a pile of unread magazines, and moved her rocking chair to a new position closer to the fireplace.

Flanagan watched her warily. Only his eyes moved, though; he'd planted his chin on his front paws, and he seemed to be pretending to be invisible.

She sat down finally, to contemplate a new position for the couch. There wasn't much to do except think, since the couch was too big and heavy for her to shift by herself and there was still no sign of movement from the office.

She put her head down on an overstuffed cushion. Whatever was going on in there, she thought, it had better not be baseball scores or surefire stock buys. Or dowries, either.

She'd closed her eyes for just a moment, she was certain—but the next thing she heard was Ridge's voice. "You've got ten seconds before I give you the Sleeping Beauty treatment, Morea."

She sat up so suddenly that her muscles snapped like rubber bands. "Don't threaten me like that, Coltrain." Too late, she remembered that her father might well be listening, and she bit her lip hard and looked around for him.

Ridge was leaning over her, almost blocking her view of the room. "If you're going to be nasty, next time I'll only give you five seconds' warning." He sat down on the edge of the couch next to her. "Are you always this feisty when you first wake up?"

Somewhat blearily, Morea focused her eyes on her wristwatch. "It's almost midnight, and you have the nerve to ask me that?"

"Good thing I sent your dad home before I started

shaking you, wouldn't you say? By the way, he obviously thought I knew what to expect when you regained consciousness—as if I've been observing the phenomenon regularly.''

Morea groaned. "I *told* him we weren't sleeping together!''

"Well, he obviously didn't believe you.''

"And you didn't help matters by throwing him out at this hour, and staying yourself, did you?'' She thought better of the accusation and added irritably, "But I'll admit it was probably wise of you to dispense with Daddy.''

"A bit ungracious, as apologies go, but I suppose it'll have to do.''

"And as for that threat to kiss me, remember? You promised you wouldn't do that again.''

"Oh, no. I promised I wouldn't kiss you casually. Shocking you awake is a whole different matter.'' Ridge settled onto the edge of the couch, trapping her. "Is this how you prepare for a case, Morea? I always wondered what your secret was.''

She stuck her tongue out at him. "My briefcase was in the office with you, so I could hardly do anything useful.''

"Shortsighted of you. Too bad I didn't spot it. I might have found it interesting, especially if you left anything in there about the Madisons' settlement.''

"I didn't. Anyway, you're the one who said I needed a little distraction tonight, not more work.''

His eyes narrowed slightly, and his gaze roamed over her face, then down her body with a slow thoroughness which made Morea's breath catch in her throat.

What was he seeing? The remnants of sleep, obviously—rosy cheeks, heavy eyelids, and hair wildly out of place. But did he find those telltale signs an attraction or a turnoff? There was something about the way he was looking at her...

She had to fight the urge to pat her hair back into place. To do anything of the sort would tell him that she wasn't indifferent to his survey...

And you're not indifferent, are you? whispered a sly little voice in the back of her mind. *If he wanted to kiss you, right now...*

"It appears we did the trick," Ridge said. "As a matter of fact, you look very distracted."

The familiar note of lazy humor was back in his voice, but there was something else underneath, something Morea couldn't quite define. Was it surprise? Irony? Sardonic enjoyment of the reaction he'd caused?

She ought not to care, of course, even if he was laughing at her instead of with her—but she did, somehow. There was no time to sort out the reasons just now, however; Ridge's gaze had focused more tightly on her face, and Morea let her chin drop. "Did you get him to talk?"

"Talk? The main trouble I've had with your father is getting him to shut up."

"Well? What did you find out?"

"For one thing, I discovered that I'm starving."

"Tough. I offered you dinner once and you turned it down."

Ridge looked wounded.

In fact, Morea thought uncharitably, at the moment he looked a bit like Flanagan. The resemblance lay in the enormous, sad eyes, she decided.

"That was hours ago," Ridge said. "And I've done a lot of hard work since."

"You sound pathetic, Coltrain. Oh, all right—raid the refrigerator."

He didn't wait for a second invitation. She listened to him rattle around in her kitchen for a few minutes and finally followed, settling herself on a high stool at the breakfast bar to watch as he made himself a sandwich with her last three slices of ham. He paused with a hunk of cheese suspended over the plate and said, "I'm not robbing you of tomorrow's lunch, am I?"

"I wasn't planning to brown-bag, no."

"That's good. I'd hate to think of you being as hungry tomorrow as I am tonight. Even though giving up your food is all in a good cause."

She'd slid off her stool to get a bag of chips from the cupboard, and she paused with the package in her hand. "Then he did tell you?"

"He told me."

Morea ripped the cellophane and dumped the chips into a bowl. Her fingers shook slightly. "And...?"

"You know the rules, Morea." He put the mustard jar back in the refrigerator and gathered up his sandwich.

"You mean you're not going to tell me?"

Ridge looked at her quizzically. "Do you stop thinking in legal terms after midnight, or what? I can't tell anybody anything without Charles' permission—which I haven't got, particularly where you're concerned."

"He's my father, dammit!"

"And he's my client, so—"

Morea's annoyance spilled over. "Well, not for long. As soon as I find a really good attorney—"

"Good luck," Ridge said through a bite of ham and cheese. "He's going to need one. This is a honey of a case."

"Oh, that's really helpful." *And frightening*, she thought. But something kept her from admitting to Ridge how overwhelmingly scared she was.

"I suggested he tell you, because your feminine view of things might come in handy. Or, if he didn't want to confess, he could let me fill you in. He said he'd think about it. But in the meantime, my hands are tied.''

Rhetorical though the reference had been, Morea found herself staring at his hands. Long-fingered, lean, sun-browned—they were confident hands. Strong hands. Hands that could be trusted to safely hold anything from a ham sandwich to a life.

She sighed. ''All right,'' she said reluctantly. ''I guess I don't have any choice but to continue to play dumb. But if there's anything I can do—''

''Anything?'' He polished off the last crumb of the sandwich and thoughtfully licked a dab of mustard off his index finger. ''Well, as long as you've asked, there is something, as a matter of fact.''

His tone warned her; it was just a little too bland, too casual, too nonchalant. ''And what exactly do you have in mind, Coltrain?''

''Gee, you're a suspicious sort,'' Ridge said plaintively. ''You sound like I'd asked you to go to bed with me, as a bribe.''

A wave of color flooded Morea's face.

''When all I really wanted to ask was if you happen to have any ice cream. A little taste of chocolate would finish off that meal in grand style.''

''No ice cream.''

''Does that mean you don't have any, or you won't share? Never mind—I know when I'm not welcome.'' He raised his voice slightly. ''Flanagan, the lady has indicated that we should leave now.''

The dog woke with a snuffle and got reluctantly to his feet. He trailed Ridge to the door, but he kept one sleepy eye on Morea. He looked as if he was hoping for an invitation to stay.

No doubt about it, she thought. *It's a lot more peaceful here than on Rowena's porch!*

At the front door, Ridge paused, and Morea braced herself for another salvo. "I thought you couldn't work because your briefcase was in the office." He pointed to the black leather bag, half-hidden in the shadow of the hallway.

Morea looked at it in astonishment. "Oh. I forgot, I guess. Dad came upstairs with me, and we went straight through to the kitchen. I thought I'd put it in the office as I usually do."

Ridge leaned against the doorjamb and looked down at her with concern. "You know, I'm worried about you, Morea. Probably the next thing you'll forget is that this scheme of your mother's is only make-believe, and—"

"Don't lose any sleep over that possibility."

Ridge didn't seem to hear. "Then you'll start acting as if we're really serious about each other—"

"Not a chance, Coltrain."

"And I'll no doubt end up having to marry you after all."

Morea was speechless.

He shook his head. "The only alternative would be to squash your illusions," he said earnestly, "and if I did that, I'd drown myself in guilt for the rest of my life. No, there's no help for it that I can see. And don't worry, darling—it's all right, really. I'll just have to make the sacrifice." Gently, he brushed his hand down her cheek, smiled sadly, and was gone.

CHAPTER SEVEN

MOREA had lunch on Friday in the firm's executive dining room, hoping to catch George Bradley to ask if he'd had any further thoughts about the best attorney to represent her father. But eventually, when he didn't show up, she finished her chicken salad and started back to her office. She'd dawdled as long as she could, and the Madisons' settlement conference was due to start. This time she wasn't about to give Ridge the satisfaction of being late.

On her way out of the dining room, however, she ran into Alan Davis, who greeted her with a smile and drew her aside into the hallway. "I haven't seen you all week," he began.

"It's been a busy one, and it's not over by any means. As a matter of fact, I have an appointment right now, so—"

"I'll walk you back to your office, then." Alan dropped into step beside her. "You're going to George Bradley's cocktail party tomorrow night, aren't you?"

"I didn't even know he was having one."

"It's shorter notice than usual. The invitations were just delivered this morning, but I'm sure you'll have gotten one."

"Just what I need, another event pushed onto a crowded calendar. And not only is it on a weekend, but it's one of the few I'd managed to keep relatively free this summer."

Alan took a deep breath. "I guess there's no point in asking you to go with me, is there?"

Morea shook her head. Maybe the man was learning, after all.

"All right—at least I can see you there. By the way, Trent Paxton tells me he really likes you."

Win a few, lose a few, Morea thought. She'd still been cherishing a faint hope that after he had a few days to think about it, Trent Paxton would prefer a different attorney. "I can't think why. I force-fed him a whole lot of unpalatable truths."

"Well, he was still singing your praises when I ran into him at the gym last night. You're obviously a hit."

Morea paused in the corridor outside her office suite and looked up at Alan. "No thanks to you," she said coolly, "after you as much as told him I'd get him off cheap."

Alan looked stunned. "Good heavens, Morea, what's hit you?"

"You don't even see the problem, do you? If I'd brought a client to you and told him what you'd do with his case before you'd even had a chance to hear the circumstances, you'd have been screaming all the way to top management. So don't ever again put me in the position of having to contradict what you've already told a client, or I guarantee I'll dump the mess right back in your lap."

Alan shrugged. "All right, all right, but I think you're overstating things. All I said was you'd make sure he didn't pay any more than necessary. Of course he doesn't want to be taken for a ride. His wife is—"

Morea interrupted. "Entitled to a fair settlement. Sorry if that concept upsets you, Alan, but my job—"

His mouth tightened. "Your job isn't to look after the opposition, it's to do the best you can for our client."

Morea nodded. "Exactly. And the best service I can do for Trent Paxton is to put together a fair settlement that will keep him out of court in the future. If he pinches pennies now, he may be fighting this battle for years.''

''Well, that's no reason to give away a fortune.''

''I said fair—and I meant fair to both parties.''

Morea started to push open the door to her office suite, but a masculine hand reached past her to do so. It was a long-fingered hand, strong and brown, with a snowy white shirt cuff peeking out from under the sleeve of a tan sports coat—a hand and arm as far unlike Alan's plump white fingers and navy pinstripes as it was possible to get.

She didn't even look up, just said with resignation, ''Hello, Ridge. You're early.''

''Only because I couldn't stand to wait another moment to see you, my beloved.''

His voice was low and intimate and caressing, and Morea saw Alan's eyes widen with shock. ''Have you two met?'' she said, and introduced them. ''And don't take him seriously, Alan,'' she added. ''He'd probably say the same thing to you if he thought it would keep you off balance.''

''Now that's an idea,'' Ridge agreed. He smiled at Alan and let the office door swing shut so he could shake hands. ''I'll keep it in reserve for a moment when I really need an advantage, though.''

Alan muttered something and hurried away.

''One would think I was contagious,'' Ridge murmured. He looked quizzically down at Morea. ''I hope you're planning to apply that philosophy of yours about fair settlements and the downside of penny-pinching to the Madisons, as well as to...what was that name? Paxton?''

''You expect me to tell you?''

''I suppose not. How did your case go yesterday?''

"Is that a social-type question, or do you really care?"

"But of course I care!" The corner of Ridge's mouth quirked. "I'd hate to see you fall apart in court against anyone but me."

"Well, I didn't fall apart. I was great, and I triumphed."

With the swiftness of mercury, Ridge shifted tactics. "See? I told you distraction would be a good idea."

Morea burst into laughter. "Don't you ever give up?"

"Not if I can help it."

"Well, you certainly distracted me that night. In fact, the effect has lasted. I woke up about four o'clock this morning half-convinced that I'd actually married you after all." She smiled sweetly up at him. "It was the most horrendous nightmare I've ever experienced."

"Poor darling. Too bad you were alone...you *were* alone, weren't you? I wasn't there to comfort you?"

"In *your* dreams, Coltrain."

"Well, I didn't think I could have forgotten that sort of episode," he said thoughtfully. He didn't give her a chance to answer before he pushed the door open again and flashed a smile at her secretary. "Hello, Cindy. You won't believe how much I've missed you. If you ever get tired of the luxuries of working for Morea and you want to experience the gritty world of real law—"

Morea interrupted. "And take along copies of all my case files, I suppose?"

"Of course not. Do you honestly think I'd do anything so low and underhanded as asking your secretary to steal case files?"

For an instant, Morea wasn't quite sure if the indignation in his voice was real or manufactured; she'd never seen Ridge react so strongly to any comment. But then she couldn't remember ever before hitting quite so closely to his ethical standards, either.

"Well, I wouldn't. Besides, Cindy wouldn't need to steal the files," he added slyly. "I trust her to remember all the important stuff without a paper reminder."

Cindy laughed. "Thanks for the confidence, Ridge. I'll keep you in mind if I'm ever looking for a job."

"She won't be if I have any choice in the matter," Morea said firmly. "Cindy's the best legal secretary I've ever had."

"I only try to steal the best," Ridge murmured.

"Mr. and Mrs. Madison are already in the conference room," Cindy said. "They arrived almost at the same time, about ten minutes ago. I offered them coffee, but they both refused."

"Just as well," Morea said. "They'd probably have thrown it at each other."

"Well, if you're offering me some," Ridge said, "I won't turn you down. Shall we go in now, Morea, or wait till the blood's had a chance to dry?"

Morea didn't bother to answer. She took the folder Cindy held out and led the way to the conference room.

Kathy Madison was seated primly on the far side of the oval table, with her back to the window. Across from her, lounging in his chair, was her soon-to-be-ex-husband.

The silence in the room could be sliced, Morea thought. Of course that was no surprise; she'd had divorce cases where any encounter between the spouses was so tense Morea herself had ended up with a headache.

"Let's get started," she said brightly, patting Kathy Madison's shoulder in greeting. She pulled out the chair next to her client's. "I think we've all agreed that the problem of the business is the most important to solve, and that's the issue I'd like to start with today. So if you have anything new to put on the table, Ridge..."

He took a moment to stir the coffee Cindy had just set by his elbow. "In the spirit of fairness," he said, "and with the desire not to be seen as penny-pinching—"

Morea wanted to stick her tongue out at him. Ridge knew it, too; that was obvious from the twinkle in his eyes.

The compromise he suggested, however, was a reasonable one—more reasonable, in fact, than Morea had expected—and within an hour they'd all agreed on the details. Grateful that the thorniest problem was behind them, Morea sneaked a glance at her wristwatch. With any luck they could wrap up the rest of the negotiations just as quickly...

That, of course, was before Bill pointed out that a pair of candlesticks was missing from the inventory of the house he and Kathy had shared.

"Candlesticks?" Morea asked. "You mean like candelabra?"

"No. Just crystal candle holders." Bill Madison jerked his head toward Kathy. "See? She knows what I'm talking about."

Morea glanced at her client.

Kathy had turned slightly pink. "So I overlooked the candlesticks when I wrote the inventory," she said defensively. "They're very ordinary old candlesticks. And they're not crystal, they're just glass."

Morea counted to five. She'd give Kathy a quick lecture later about the dangers of *overlooking* even the most minute bit of property—and make sure, at the same time, that nothing else had been missed.

"And you want them, Bill?" Morea asked. "Are they a family treasure, or something?"

"You could say that," Bill agreed.

"They are not," Kathy snapped.

"So if they're so ordinary, why not let me have them?"

"Because you don't deserve them!"

Morea met Ridge's gaze. His face was impassive, but she thought there was a hint of puzzlement in his eyes, as if he'd never heard of the candlesticks before, either.

She felt a tinge of relief ooze through her veins. If he'd been blindsided, too, it meant that at least he hadn't help engineer this surprise. Though she couldn't quite see why it should make a difference.

"They're a pair?" Ridge said. "Exactly the same?"

Kathy nodded.

"Then it's easy. Each of you takes one candlestick, and—"

"No!" Kathy's suddenly-strident soprano and Bill's firm baritone rang out in perfect unison.

Morea looked from one of them to the other. Kathy was blinking hard, as if she was fighting back tears. Bill's jaw was set more firmly than she'd ever seen it. "If this isn't a family treasure," she began, "why not—"

"They're a treasure to me." Kathy gave a tiny sniff. "And that's the only reason he wants them, too. To hurt me."

Bill shook his head. "Who cares if it hurts you? I always liked those candlesticks. Besides, I'm the one who found them."

"Well, I'm the one who paid for them!"

"With money that was a gift to us both. Wedding money. Remember?"

Morea began to see the light. "On your honeymoon, no doubt?"

Kathy nodded. "We found them in a little junk shop in San Diego. They were filthy."

"Which is why you didn't want them," Bill pointed out. "You said they'd never clean up, so I soaked them for a week when we got home."

"And I told you how to do it, with vinegar and water—"

Morea held up a hand. The last thing they needed was a lecture on household hints. Better to defuse the situation and hope that the battling Madisons would cool down. "Let's leave the candlesticks for later discussion and move on to the rest of the undecided property."

"No," Kathy said stubbornly. "The candlesticks come first, because either I get them, or I'm not agreeing to Bill having another single thing."

"All right," Ridge said gently. "You take the candlesticks, and Bill gets everything else on the disputed list."

"Wait a minute," Morea began. "I can't allow—"

Bill shook his head firmly. "Nope. No deal. I want the candlesticks. I saw them first, and they're mine by rights."

Ridge glanced at him. "Then Kathy gets everything else on the list."

"No," Kathy said. "I won't settle for that."

Morea wanted to scream. "You're both acting like adolescents, you know."

Ridge's eyebrows rose in astonishment.

All right, Morea thought, *maybe I shouldn't have said it*. But now that she had, she couldn't back down—and she had no desire to, anyway, because it was the truth. She snapped, "As I see it, Ridge, part of my job is to point out the facts, whether or not the client likes them. And in this case—"

"In this case," Ridge said crisply, "I'll take care of

telling my client when he's acting like a spoiled child. Bill, you're acting like a spoiled child.''

Kathy's chin went up. "You just don't understand. Those are very special candlesticks!''

Morea could hardly believe her ears. Surely Kathy wasn't defending her husband…was she?

"Then you take one each,'' Ridge said. "It's a sensible compromise.''

The Madisons sounded like a country-music duet. "Never.''

Morea threw up her hands. "Obviously this isn't going anywhere. You're paying us by the hour while you argue over petty property. Kathy, I'll buy you another set of candlesticks—''

"No other set would do,'' Kathy said.

"And it's not petty property, Ms. Landon,'' Bill said.

Morea's jaw dropped. She couldn't recall Bill Madison ever speaking directly to her before, in any of their conferences. For him to have chosen that moment and that subject… One would think he was standing up for Kathy.

For a full half-minute, the conference room was silent, except for a single sniff from Kathy.

Bill said, "Ms. Landon is right about one thing, though. Kathy, it's costing us a fortune to sit here. Do you suppose we could talk about some of this by ourselves?''

Kathy didn't look at him. Instead she reached for a tissue and defiantly blew her nose. "We haven't had much luck at that so far, have we? What makes you think it would be any different now?''

The bitter ache in her voice left a metallic taste in Morea's mouth.

Nobody answered. Kathy sniffed again. "Oh, why not? I hate sitting here and being called a spoiled child.''

With difficulty, Morea refrained from pointing out that it was Bill, not Kathy, who'd been on the receiving end of that particular description.

"If you two think you can come to an agreement," Ridge said, "I'm all for it."

Morea said, "You don't have to settle everything, either. Just make notes on anything you decide on, and we'll set up a time when you can bring back your conclusions and run through them all together."

Morea was still jotting a note in her calendar for their appointment the following week when the Madisons left the conference room. From the corner of her eye, she noted that Bill, with icy politeness, held the door for Kathy, who stepped carefully aside so she wouldn't brush against him.

"Well," Ridge said. "Do you suppose they'll ever come back?"

"Of course they will." She didn't even look at him. "At the rate they're going, they can't possibly settle anything."

"Unless they go after each other with the candlesticks. That could be pretty final."

"Surely you don't think they would." Morea paused. "On the other hand..."

"Maybe it's a good thing Kathy hid the things."

"She said she overlooked them."

"I'll bet," Ridge said rudely. "And I suppose she didn't remember them because they're tucked under a pile of worn-out clothes in the darkest corner of the basement—or somewhere equally unlikely."

"Things do get put away out of sight sometimes."

"Particularly when there's a divorce pending."

"Like you've never had a client who pulled a silly stunt!"

Ridge yawned and leaned back in his chair. "It just

goes to show the importance of a good prenuptial agreement.''

"How's that?" Morea scoffed. "They bought the damned candlesticks on the honeymoon, so they couldn't have been listed in any prenuptial contract.''

"All honeymoon souvenirs will be purchased in pairs,'' Ridge decreed, "one for each party. See? If it's decided right up front, there's nothing to argue about. I'll remember to put that into the next draft of our prenuptial agreement.''

"Don't waste your time.''

"You sound almost like a romantic, Morea.'' Ridge stretched lazily. "Do you mean you think we shouldn't bother with a contract?''

"Of course not.'' Belatedly, as he started to smile, Morea heard the ambiguity in her words. She wanted to swear; she couldn't have been lucky enough for Ridge to miss something like that. "If I was getting married, of course I'd want a prenuptial agreement. But that kind of clause is pretty cold—splitting up the souvenirs before the honeymoon's even over practically assures that the marriage won't last. Talk about assuming the worst—''

Ridge had put his head back against the leather chair. His eyes were no more than narrow slits, as if he were half-asleep.

Morea wondered if he was too comfortable to move, so he was keeping up the conversational jabs just to keep her from throwing him out of the conference room.

His voice was as slow as syrup on a cold afternoon. "Do you mean a couple of years in this business hasn't made you a complete cynic after all?''

"Thinking that all marriages are bound to end in court? There's a difference between realism and cynicism, Ridge.''

He sat up a little straighter. "How do you manage to

do this every day, anyway?'' He sounded honestly curious. "I hate messy divorces. It's stressful enough to have to deal with battling couples once in a while, but if that's all my whole practice consisted of…''

"I do other things, too—family law things. And I look at divorce as a necessary evil. It's bad enough that it exists, but if I can help a couple get through the legalities without wounding each other for life, I've accomplished something worthwhile.''

There was a long silence. Then Ridge gave a soft, low whistle.

Morea stared suspiciously at him. "What does that mean, Coltrain?''

"I was just thinking how much I like this new, visionary you,'' he murmured.

Morea blinked in confusion, completely taken aback. But of course, that was Ridge's specialty, wasn't it?— zeroing in on her weakest spot with a totally unexpected line of attack?

Don't take him seriously, she warned herself. *Not that you want to, anyway.*

"That's in general, of course,'' she went on. Her voice was surprisingly level. "But I have to admit that sessions like this one are enough to put me off marriage altogether.''

"Too true,'' Ridge drawled, and stood up slowly. "Well, I wish I could say it's been a thoroughly enjoyable afternoon, love, but—''

"I'm glad you're not going to perjure yourself, Ridge.''

He grinned. "Next time let's not invite the Madisons, okay? In the meantime, at least we have tea to look forward to on Sunday.''

"Ridge, surely now that Daddy's confided in you, we

don't have to go through with that bit of play-acting. Do we?''

"It's up to you, pet. I suppose I could call Charles up and mention that you engineered the whole scam just to manipulate him. He might have developed enough trust in me to let that little issue pass, but—"

Morea groaned. "See you Sunday."

"That's what I thought," Ridge murmured, and was gone.

Morea had set aside the entire afternoon for the Madison conference, so with its unexpectedly early end, she had a couple of hours unscheduled. She flipped through her mail and messages and stopped to read the invitation to George Bradley's home for a Saturday cocktail party.

Of all the inane events the human race had ever invented, Morea thought cocktail parties must rank at the head of the list. Particularly the business-related ones which provided just another opportunity to see the same people one worked with every day. And to schedule it on a weekend, as if no one in the firm had any other interest besides work...

The only good thing, Morea thought, was that she'd have another chance to ask George about the attorneys he'd mentioned, and see if he'd found out anything which made one a better choice than another. At least she could present Ridge with a short list of names, so he'd be prepared once Charles decided to fight.

As he would, Morea told herself firmly. The idea that he still might opt for what seemed to be an easier way wasn't even to be considered. Charles wasn't a quitter; he wouldn't simply resign.

In addition to the cocktail-party invitation, there was a stack of messages. She flipped through them, automatically sorting critical from less important, until she came to a pink slip which said simply, "Synnamon Welles wants you to call her." There were three phone numbers listed.

"She wasn't sure where she'd be," Cindy said, "so she gave me home, office, and cellular."

"Any idea which order I should try them in?"

Cindy shook her head. "I'd flip a coin for you, but I don't have one with three sides."

"You," Morea warned, "have been hanging around with Ridge Coltrain entirely too much." Cindy grinned, and Morea went back into her office.

Synnamon's secretary said, rather vaguely, that she'd left the office some time ago. The only answer at her apartment was an answering machine. The cellular phone rang a half-dozen times; Morea was about to give up when it clicked, and Synnamon—sounding a bit distracted—said hello.

"Sorry if I caught you at a bad time," Morea said.

"Well, I can't exactly chat at the moment. I just wanted to tell you that I talked to the dean of students at the university, and there are three sets of files waiting for you in his office."

Morea was aghast. "*Three*? You mean there's been more than one complaint?"

"Against your father? Heavens, no—I'm sorry to shake you up. I couldn't think of a way to single out just one student, so I narrowed it down as much as possible and told him I'd send my attorney in to look over the files."

Morea's heartbeat steadied. "Well, that's a relief. You told him about the scholarship?"

"I sort of hinted at the idea, but I tried to leave you as much maneuvering room as possible. And I didn't give him your name, either."

"That's probably good. How did you manage that

kind of access, anyway? I didn't think we had a prayer of seeing the actual files, or I'd have never bothered with the notion of the scholarship in the first place.''

"You don't want to know how I did it," Synnamon said darkly. "Sorry, darling—I have to run."

She sounded almost breathless, Morea thought. "Are you all right? What's the matter? Are you in the middle of a traffic jam?"

"No—though come to think of it, I sort of feel as if I've been hit by a car."

Suspiciously, Morea asked, "Exactly where are you, Synnamon?"

"In the hospital. I ought to have known as soon as I found a project that interested me, this baby would take a notion to be ten days early."

"You're having a baby and you're talking to me?"

"Don't worry, they tell me I'm still only in the first stage. Though if this is what early labor feels like—" Synnamon's voice rose to a near wail. "I...want... drugs!"

Morea could feel a sympathetic sweat breaking out on her own forehead. "Is there anything I can do?"

After a moment when all she could hear was panting, Synnamon said, "As a matter of fact, yes. Trading places with me would be really thoughtful of you. I'll happily go read student files while you—"

"Tell you what," Morea said hastily, "I'll stop by this evening to see how you're doing."

"Some friend you are," Synnamon grumbled. "Chickening out the minute I ask for one *teensy* little favor in return for everything I've ever done for you... Dammit, here comes another one. Better save that visit for tomorrow—the nurses say this might go on for a while. 'Bye, Morea."

Morea's hands were shaking when she put the telephone down. What on earth made a woman put herself through that sort of agony, with no end in sight? Morea was no coward, but she couldn't fathom deliberately taking on such pain in order to give a man the son he wanted. No matter how much she loved him...

The power of love, she thought. She'd never understand it.

Morea intended to go directly home from the university. But instead she drove straight to downtown Denver as if the BMW was on autopilot, and when she found herself at the entrance to Taylor Bradley Cummings' parking ramp she shrugged and pulled in. She'd packed her briefcase in a hurry and had left behind some papers. If she picked them up now, she could work at home this weekend.

Instead of taking the elevator to her office, however, she went around the corner to Ridge's. She might as well tell him what she'd found.

This time a well-groomed older woman occupied the desk in the outer office, and when Morea introduced herself, her eyes brightened. "I'm sure he'll want to see you," she said. "Go on in."

Morea gave a hesitant tap and pushed the door open. She couldn't see him. "Ridge? If it's not a convenient time for you..."

He appeared from behind the door, a law book open in his hands. He'd stripped off jacket and tie and rolled his shirt sleeves to his elbows, and Morea noted the way each separate muscle in his forearms stood out under the tanned skin. The book he was holding with such apparent casualness must weigh ten pounds.

"Hi. At least your timing isn't inconvenient, let's put it that way. And since you're not likely to find me doing anything embarrassing in my office, you don't have to hover behind the door till I collect myself, either.''

Why that should make her feel tongue-tied was more than Morea could understand. She closed the door behind her and sat down in the chair next to his desk, remembering just a moment too late how uncomfortable it was. "Of course you're not doing anything embarrassing,'' she said. "The state your furniture is in, if you tried to seduce a woman in this office you'd end up a quadriplegic.''

"There is always the carpet, of course,'' Ridge murmured. "It may be slightly threadbare but it's clean. I shampooed it myself before I moved my stuff in.'' He sat down, his chair creaking ominously. "What can I do for you? Oh, excuse me—I should offer you refreshments. We don't run to china coffee services, I'm afraid, but…'' He pulled open a drawer and tugged out an opened package of taco chips. "I'll see if Marian can find a teabag, though.'' He held out the taco chips.

Morea shook her head. "Don't bother with tea, and I never eat taco chips. I found out what's in that student's academic file.'' With a tinge of conscience, she added, "Or I should say, Synnamon did.''

Ridge's eyes brightened. "And—''

"And nothing, I'm afraid. She's absolutely squeaky clean. Basically a good academic record, and great recommendations from professors at her former college.''

Ridge didn't answer. He picked up his fountain pen from the desk blotter and rolled it absently between his hands as he leaned back in his chair. "That's Synnamon's opinion, of course?''

"No—I read the file myself. She just got access for me.''

"Oh. I was hoping…''

"That she might have missed something—I know. I

went over it word by word. It's good, Ridge. That student's not going to be easy to discredit.''

"Well, I'd rather be warned about that now than after we get into court.'' He reached for a taco chip and crunched it thoughtfully between strong white teeth.

"*If* we get into court," Morea said. "I guess I see now why Daddy's considering resigning instead.'' Then something about the tone of Ridge's voice struck home. "You mean he's *agreed*?''

"He called a while ago to tell me he's thought over our discussion, and he's decided not to resign."

Morea was around the desk before Ridge had managed to return his chair to the upright position. She flung her arms out in an exuberant, congratulatory hug. "I knew you could convince him to fight! I knew it!''

The spiky heel of her left shoe caught on a loose seam in the carpet, throwing her weight awkwardly atop Ridge. The heavy chair, already off balance, tipped slowly and inexorably backward. Morea fought to free herself, but it was too late; one of her hands was caught between Ridge's neck and the back of the chair; the other closed uselessly on the front of his shirt.

Only the sheer size of the chair prevented the back of Ridge's head from being slammed against the floor. Morea's forehead banged his chin as she came to rest atop him.

The sound of the collision seemed to echo.

"Thanks for your confidence," Ridge said. "But—'' He sounded a little breathless, as if the impact with either the floor or Morea herself had knocked all the air out of him. Morea wouldn't have been surprised; she was feeling a bit short of oxygen, too.

The office door swung open abruptly and the secretary appeared. "Ridge, what on earth are you doing—'' She stopped and peered over the desk, and Morea saw her gaze flicker in astonishment.

Morea's hands were pinned under Ridge's shoulders, preventing her from getting enough leverage to push herself up. She could feel the hem of her skirt cutting into her thigh, a whole lot higher than the designer had intended. She'd lost one of her shoes along the way, and Ridge's shirtfront was open; her cheek was nestled against the mat of curly dark hair on his chest. She vaguely remembered hearing the rip of fabric as she'd grabbed for support.

"Excuse me," the secretary said primly, and backed out.

Morea swore under her breath and struggled to push herself free.

Ridge's arm closed around her and held her still. "As I was starting to say, Morea, darling," he murmured into her ear. "I didn't realize you *wanted* to try out the carpet. Why on earth didn't you just tell me?"

CHAPTER EIGHT

THIS, Morea thought, had to be the most undignified
position she'd ever occupied, in all her twenty-seven
years.

Ridge's breath tickled her ear. His arm curved around
her back—comfortingly warm but as weighty as a sand-
bag, pressing her into the length of his body. Her arms
had begun to prickle from lack of circulation. She raised
her head a fraction—as far as she was able. She couldn't
quite meet his gaze, but she could count the fine pores
in his skin and detect the first signs of five o'clock
shadow along his jawline.

There was absolutely no reason for her sudden urge
to rub a fingertip over that slight stubble, or press her
lips against the strong jaw, or simply relax and melt even
more closely against his body... Or perhaps there was a
very logical reason.

It's an automatic hormonal response, she told herself
flatly. *The kind of thing any woman would feel, caught
in this position. And the sooner I get out of this spot,
the better.*

"Short of a crane," Morea said tartly, "do you have
any suggestions about how we extricate ourselves from
this position?"

"You mean you want to get out? I was just looking
for a way to be slightly more comfortable, myself." But
Ridge moved his arm enough for Morea to shift her
weight, and then, one-handed and without apparent effort, lifted her till she could get her feet untangled and
clamber off him.

She didn't look at him. As Ridge got to his feet,

Morea fumbled around for her missing shoe, trying at the same time to smooth the wrinkles out of her linen skirt. The combination threatened her balance, and only Ridge's hand on her arm kept her from stumbling again.

"Sorry," she muttered. "I'm just a little dizzy."

"Really? You had that effect on me, too."

Morea glared at him. "It must have been the way I hit my head."

"Of course it was," Ridge murmured. He lifted the heavy chair upright and sat down cautiously, hands braced on the edge of the desk in case he needed to catch himself. "My chair seems to be all right, so I don't think there's any serious harm done."

No harm? Morea thought. *Well, maybe we didn't hurt the chair.* But at the moment she felt she herself would never be quite the same again.

"That chair," she said acidly, "has probably not been all right in the last ten years. Maybe twenty."

"But you must admit it adds a certain element of interest to my office. Isn't that what expensive decorators are always trying to accomplish? Now, what were you saying before you tried to destroy my chair?"

He didn't need to make it sound as if she'd planned that episode, Morea thought irritably. Only by reminding herself that he was trying to provoke a reaction was she able to gather up the last bits of her dignity and refuse to gratify him. "I've forgotten." She perched on the edge of her own chair, suddenly unwilling to trust anything in the entire office which possessed legs.

And that includes Ridge, she thought. He'd seemed perfectly content to lie there and pretend he could hardly move, much less lift her, until she'd protested—and then he'd managed it without the slightest trouble.

He also hadn't bothered to rebutton his shirt, she noted, and she was having difficulty keeping her eyes off the wedge of tanned, hairy chest which was visible under the snowy white fabric.

"Well, I haven't forgotten," Ridge said. "You were congratulating me, and I thought you'd found a particularly delightful way to express your gratitude. Now I suppose I'll have to settle for that steak dinner after all."

Morea said, "I don't owe you a steak dinner. But I'm sure you'll pout and nag—"

"I *never* pout and nag."

"And maybe even harass me with a lawsuit if I hold out—"

Ridge nodded approvingly. "Now you've got it. That's much more my style. It was a verbal contract, and you're obligated—"

"It was not any sort of contract, but I'll buy you dinner anyway. Where do you want to go?"

"The Pinnacle."

"But that's my favorite—" Morea paused. That was odd. Why didn't she want to go to the Pinnacle with Ridge? He could have insisted on some dive where she'd be really uncomfortable.

"It's either that or Emilio's," he added. "It's got no atmosphere, but the burgers and steaks are great."

In other words, it's a dive, Morea thought. "I've never heard of it."

"Really? Of course, Emilio's is in Phoenix, but—"

"Then it will have to be the Pinnacle," Morea said sweetly. "Because I promised to stop by the hospital tonight, and I couldn't be back from Phoenix in time."

Ridge frowned. "What's at the hospital? Do you expect to need your stomach pumped?"

"From a dinner at the Pinnacle? Bite your tongue."

She tried not to watch as he rebuttoned his shirt, unfolded the rolled-up sleeves and fastened the cuffs, and knotted his tie. Each motion was smooth and efficient, but oddly sensual, as well. Morea was certain he didn't realize the way his fingers stroked the fine fabrics, but the movement of his hands sent shivers over her body as if he were touching her skin instead of cotton and raw silk, bringing back memories of the heat of his body pressed against her own.

What an idiot you are, she told herself. *That whole episode was purely an accident.*

"Fortunately," Ridge said lightly, giving the tie one last pat, "this covers up the rips where you practically tore the buttons off my shirt. For shame, Morea." He slung his jacket over his shoulder and held the door for her. The secretary was gone, and the lights were off in the outer office.

Ridge didn't look surprised at the defection; he merely dug a set of keys from the depths of his pocket and locked the door. "No doubt Marian didn't dare come in to say goodnight to us for fear of what might be going on."

Morea pretended not to hear him.

The sun was dropping in the western sky, turning the distant mountains into shimmering red and purple. From street level, as they walked the couple of blocks to the Pinnacle, they could catch only glimpses, but from the restaurant, located atop one of Denver's tallest hotels, the view would be perfect.

If, Morea thought, they didn't have to wait too long for a table. Early as it was for the dinner crowd, there were already half a dozen couples waiting for the elevator to the rooftop.

In the Pinnacle's lobby, as they waited for the maître d's attention, Morea craned her neck in an attempt to see the ever-shifting panorama of light and shadow against the mountainous horizon. To do so, she had to peer through the length of the bar and across the heads of a dozen early-dining patrons...

She blinked, and froze.

"What's the matter?" Ridge asked.

"I thought I saw the Madisons."

"Kathy and Bill?"

Morea nodded, but just then the maître d' turned to them with a smile. "Ms. Landon—I have a lovely table for two. Or are you expecting friends?"

"No, it's just the two of us tonight," Ridge murmured. "A very special night, so we'd like maximum privacy and no interruptions... Dammit, Morea, it *is* special; it's the first time I've ever been here. So why did you step on my foot?"

"Did I?" she cooed. "I'm so sorry. I'll aim better next time—I meant to kick your ankle."

The maître d', looking slightly puzzled, took them through to a window table which at the moment looked east over the high plains. Morea shook out her napkin. "Darn," she said. "By the time we revolve halfway around, the most beautiful part of sunset will be over."

"But at least we don't have the sun in our eyes now. Where did you think you saw the Madisons?"

"Almost opposite. I must have been mistaken, anyway."

"Well, it wouldn't be surprising if you had them on your mind, though I suppose they might have come here to talk."

"Why?"

"Because they can't yell in a place like this."

Morea was thoughtful. "That's not a bad notion, really. There are people I'd recommend the idea to—but I can't quite see the Madisons agreeing to the ground rules. They might go to Maxie's Bar, maybe, to fight it out, but not the Pinnacle." She opened her menu, glanced at it, and then looked up at him. "And what did you mean, you've never been here? You said when you made this bet that you'd already chosen the place. Something about steaks as big as roasts—which certainly implies you'd eaten there before.''

''Ah,'' Ridge said gently. ''I thought you said there wasn't a bet.''

Caught in her own web, Morea almost stuttered. ''There isn't. But—''

''Therefore, this doesn't count as paying off your losses. I'm saving my favorite place for when you decide to honor your contract.''

She glared at him. ''That is the most arrant piece of nonsense... All right, Coltrain. We're here. We'll eat, and I'll pay the bill. But I don't have to talk to you in the meantime.''

''Shades of the Madisons,'' he murmured. But, obviously unconcerned about her announcement, he glanced at his menu, laid it aside, and began to tell her about an incident which had happened in court that week.

After a couple of minutes, Morea gave up. He really *was* charming, and the story was too funny to ignore. And why should she ruin her digestion by trying to hold a grudge, anyway?

Over the appetizer, they talked art and drama. With the entrée they switched to politics. And only over dessert did Morea bring up her father's case.

''I know you can't talk in any detail about how you're going to handle this,'' she said.

''I couldn't if I wanted to,'' Ridge pointed out. ''Since I don't yet know myself.''

Morea nodded. ''But it's going to be even more difficult than we thought, isn't it? That student's record will make her a tough witness.''

''It's troubling, that's true. A jury will be likely to wonder what someone like that would have to gain from making charges in the first place if they weren't true.''

''Mother told me...'' Morea tried to recall Meredith's

exact words, but it was difficult to remember; that whole first conversation was now little more than a blur in her mind. "The student wasn't working up to standard, and Daddy had tried to help her out. But even with the slack he gave her, she still wasn't doing well enough, and finally he had to stop making excuses for her."

Ridge sounded dissatisfied. "But if she's such a good student, why should she have so much trouble?"

"Maybe she's not such a good student now. Just because she was in the past doesn't mean..." The explanation sounded lame even to her own ears. It would take something far stronger than that argument to win credibility in court.

"And giving her special treatment, then pulling the plug, doesn't look good for your father, either, Morea."

She bristled. "All I know is, if Daddy says he didn't do it, then he didn't do it!"

Ridge looked at her levelly over a bite of seven-layer fudge cake. "That's an admirable attitude for a daughter. It's not so hot for an attorney."

He was right, and Morea knew it. If she was going to be involved in this case at all, even if it was only to do research behind the scenes, she couldn't afford to lose what little objectivity she still possessed. And Ridge's questions didn't mean that he doubted Charles' word, either, she reminded herself. Every good attorney played devil's advocate, in order to anticipate and fend off the attacks against his client.

Ridge pushed away the remains of his dessert. "Earlier," he said slowly, "you sounded as if you had your doubts. You said you could understand why Charles would resign instead of fight."

"That doesn't mean I don't believe him. But it doesn't appear to be a very strong case, does it?" Ridge didn't disagree, as she'd rather hoped he would. Morea squared her shoulders and said, "Well, don't fret—I'm hoping to have a good short list of defamation attorneys by tea-time on Sunday. Then you can help Daddy choose, and you'll be out of it." She added, feeling a bit dreary, "And no doubt you'll be happy to be out of it, too."

Ridge didn't argue the point, just signaled the waiter for their check. When it arrived, he glanced at the total, tucked a couple of bills into the leather folder, and handed it back to the waiter. "Are you ready to go, Morea, or do you want another cup of coffee?"

Morea set her cup down. It was empty; she'd been cradling it just to keep her hands busy. "Dinner was supposed to be my treat, Ridge."

"Oh, it may never happen again," he assured her lightly. "But one of my clients actually paid his bill today, so I'm celebrating."

"You mean paid in honest-to-goodness cash instead of cars or chickens or whatever else you take? That *does* call for a celebration."

Ridge grinned. "Maybe I'll suggest to Bill Madison that when the time comes to settle your bill he pay you with a cartload of pennies." He offered his arm.

They'd lingered so long that they'd lost track of the restaurant's revolution and had to walk almost all the way around the circle before finding the archway to the nonrevolving central core where the elevators were located.

This time Morea got a better look, and there was no doubt of it; at a secluded table in the bar sat Kathy and Bill Madison. Even in the dim light it was apparent to Morea that Kathy had been crying.

But she wasn't crying now. The two of them were sitting very close together, and as Morea watched, Bill leaned over and put a gentle kiss on Kathy's cheek.

They were obviously too engrossed to notice anyone else, but the surprise of seeing them made Morea miss her step from the slowly-revolving platform to the stationary lobby.

She stumbled against Ridge, and only his hand under her elbow kept her from going down. "Not *again*, Morea. If you'd like to thank me for dinner, I'd be delighted, but I think the management would disapprove of you throwing yourself on top of me right here." Then he followed her gaze. "I see," he said, very slowly.

They walked back to the office tower in near-silence. Just as they reached the parking ramp, Ridge said, "Landon, are you having an identity crisis these days?"

"What do you mean?"

"Well, it begins to look as if you're not sure whether you're a divorce attorney or a marriage counselor. This is the second time in less than a year you've had a perfectly good case that's ended up in bed instead of in court."

"You don't know that Bill and Kathy are going home together."

Ridge's eyebrows arched. "Are you honestly too innocent to know the signs?"

"Of course I'm not." Morea saw the sparkle in his eyes and smothered a sigh. "I mean...." She suspected that trying to bail herself out would only get her mired deeper, so she gave it up as a lost cause. "Well, there are worse outcomes, don't you think?"

"Depends. Is this how you keep from getting discouraged by your divorce clients? Fix some of them up once in a while?"

"You know I didn't anticipate this."

"True. Who could have? I suppose it's just as well, though. I was just starting to work up my nerve to tell Bill I'd have to take myself off the case."

Morea was genuinely shocked. "Why?"

He reached over to tweak her nose. "Because one

can't be canoodling with the opposing attorney, that's why.''

She stopped dead in the middle of the parking garage. ''*Canoodling*? What a word! Besides, whatever you want to call it, we're not—and we're not likely to be, either.''

''Ah—but you know appearances. Didn't you see the looks Kathy was giving you today? She's suspicious, I'd say.''

''Well, if she is, it's your fault. Calling me up and making suggestive comments while she's right there with me—''

Ridge obviously wasn't listening. ''And then you pop into my office and start talking about seduction, and throw me on the floor, chair and all... What's a client to think? Come to that, what am *I* to think?''

Morea had never felt such a surge of embarrassment in her life. Not only her face, but her whole body felt red and steamy with the rush of hot blood. ''Dammit, Ridge, you know I didn't mean to do that.''

''Perhaps not,'' he said thoughtfully, ''but accident or not, that kind of behavior leads to all sorts of complications. Perhaps you'd like me to demonstrate?''

''Oh, no.'' Morea had already started to back away when Ridge draped an arm easily around her shoulders and pulled her against him. His other hand came to rest under her chin. His fingers splayed warmly across her throat, and the sensitive tips caressed her earlobe and the tender triangle below.

His lips were firm and gentle, asking rather than demanding. But the soft, wordless question was impossible to deny, and Morea felt the warmth of desire oozing through her veins like slow-melting butter.

She had no idea how long the kiss went on, except that it seemed forever—and, strangely enough, like no time at all. She only knew that when he raised his head, she was vaguely disappointed, and her head was spinning. She was afraid to let go of him for fear she'd reel away and fall. But she was even more afraid that if she didn't let go, she'd press herself against him and beg him to kiss her again.

She took a step backward and with relief felt a concrete pillar solid against her spine. She leaned her head against it and looked up at Ridge. The harsh yellow light of the parking garage washed away his tan; in fact, he looked just a little ill. Was that the effect of the light, or the kiss?

Perhaps, Morea thought, *he got a bit more than he bargained for.* A playful kiss had gone awry—but was he acting so stunned because of the way he'd felt, or because of Morea's response? If Ridge was shocked by his own reactions, he'd no doubt be more careful in the future, and she had nothing to worry about. If, on the other hand, he was startled by the way she'd kissed him back...

Morea didn't want to think about the questions that might lead to.

"Are you all right?" he asked.

She tried to answer, but her vocal cords didn't seem to work anymore.

The very corner of Ridge's mouth tipped upward. "Maybe stopping by a hospital isn't such a bad idea," he mused. "Perhaps they can do something to help get your voice back. I'd hate to think I'd made you permanently speechless, with nothing more than a kiss."

Morea didn't go to the hospital after all. Actually, she reflected, she hadn't exactly promised to stop by this evening—she'd only offered, and Synnamon had suggested waiting till tomorrow.

After all, it was only polite to do as her friend had asked. Tonight would probably be a terrible time, anyway. It was quite possible Synnamon would still be in labor, her child not yet born. Didn't these things go on for hours and hours sometimes, especially when it was a first pregnancy? Or, if the delivery was finished, Synnamon would be exhausted. In either case she'd hardly be in the mood for company.

Yes, Morea told herself, it would be far better to wait. It was the generous thing to do. Her hesitation to being seen in public, and by her all-knowing best friend, had absolutely nothing to do with Ridge and that sudden, shattering kiss.

Nothing.

Her apartment was cool, but the recycled air felt stale. She kicked off her shoes and opened the French doors, padding out onto the balcony.

The man could kiss; there was no doubt about that. But there was a lot of doubt in her heart about everything else. What in heaven's name had he meant about quitting the Madison case? Even if the apparent reconciliation they'd seen tonight didn't last, the settlement was practically finished, the divorce almost at an end. And there was nothing going on between Ridge and Morea which prevented each of them from giving good advice to their respective clients. To suggest otherwise was practically insulting.

And yet...

If you won't even date a partner in your own firm because it might affect your judgment, Morea asked herself, *how do you excuse that kiss?*

But she hadn't started it. Hadn't invited it. Hadn't particularly liked it...

And you're a liar, too, she accused. At least, about liking it. She'd never been quite so thoroughly kissed in her life—or come nearly so close to losing her head.

What had Ridge been thinking of, to take such a kooky action? It was almost as if he wanted an excuse to ditch Bill Madison's case. But that idea was utterly crazy.

The trouble was, the only other explanation which came to mind was crazier yet—for Morea was certainly not foolish enough to think he might actually be serious.

Synnamon's husband was standing by the big glass viewing window of the hospital nursery, absorbed in the panorama of cribs and incubators inside, when Morea came up beside him late the next afternoon.

"Hi, Conner," she said. "Is it always this much trouble to get in to see a new mother? Between questions, passes, and locked doors, I thought for a bit I'd landed in the mint instead of the hospital."

"Security," he said, absolutely deadpan. "After all, ours is the world's most incredible baby, so we have round-the-clock bodyguards and formula-tasters and—"

"Right," Morea murmured. "Which one is yours?"

"You mean you can't tell at a glimpse? Over there." He pointed at a corner crib, but the nurse bending over the side obscured the view. "Just going out to visit Mom."

Morea dropped into step beside him. She barely had time to give Synnamon a gentle hug before the baby arrived, wrapped in a pink blanket and complete with a tiny satin bow stuck in a thatch of dark hair.

"Pink?" Morea said. "I thought you said this was going to be a boy."

Synnamon blushed. "Well, you ought to know by now the kind of trouble you can get into by assuming things. I thought Conner could only be so happy if it was a boy, so—"

"But in fact, I was dying for a girl," Conner said. "With her mother's eyes and perfect skin…"

He stroked a finger down Synnamon's cheek, and for a moment, Morea was morally certain both of them had forgotten about not only their guest but their baby, snuggled at Synnamon's breast. There was something about the way they looked at one another that was unsettling—and yet perfectly delightful. It made Morea's chest ache just to watch them.

"You know, Synnamon," she said, "it's going to take a while to think of you as a mommy. I'd have just as much luck picturing myself in that role."

Which of course was out of the question. Morea Landon, high-powered attorney, with a baby? Impossible.

So why did the idea even occur to you? a sly little voice in the back of her brain murmured.

Synnamon looked up with a half-focused smile. "I don't know. Considering some of the things I've been hearing about you lately, Morea…"

Morea felt the hair on the nape of her neck rising in self-defense. "There is nothing going on between Ridge Coltrain and me."

"Funny," Synnamon murmured. "I didn't say a word about Ridge. I wonder what made you think I was talking about him."

Morea could have cheerfully bit off her tongue. What was happening to her? She'd never been so careless about what she said, even with her closest friends.

Until Ridge had come into her life like a force-five hurricane.

She stayed only a few minutes more. She didn't dare be too late for George Bradley's cocktail party. In any case, she didn't think she'd be missed; that tiny family circle was tighter now than she'd ever imagined possible. If someone had predicted this a year ago, when she'd first filed Synnamon Welles' divorce petition, Morea would have laughed herself silly. Synnamon's was to have been the perfect divorce. Instead, she'd ended up more married than ever before.

What are you, Ridge had asked last night. *A divorce attorney or a marriage counselor?*

Morea certainly took no credit for the Welles' revitalized marriage. And if Kathy and Bill Madison decided to take another stab at matrimony, it was none of Morea's doing. What did she know about marriage, anyway?

And that's enough of that, she lectured herself. *You're beginning to sound lonely and self-pitying—so get over it. Hold your head up and find something to enjoy about this party.*

George Bradley had invited not only the whole firm, but a good selection of TBC's client list, as well. Enormous though his house was, it seemed to swell with the crowd, and Morea resigned herself to an evening of straining to hear, of making small talk, of pretending interest in the dullest of conversations. She toyed with the idea of announcing something shocking just to see if anyone noticed, and gave it up reluctantly.

It's a good thing Ridge isn't here, she thought. *He'd do it in a minute.*

She almost wished he was. He'd stir things up so much that Taylor Bradley Cummings' cocktail parties would never be the same again.

She shook her head a little, trying to clear it. One would think she actually missed him!

But I do.

The thought was little more than a whisper deep in Morea's mind, so soft that it almost slipped by unnoticed. Yet she was startled to realize that despite its gentleness, the statement rang with conviction, as if it was something her subconscious had long known.

Was this why she'd felt so lonely last night, in her cool, stale, empty apartment? Was this why she'd felt so out of place this afternoon as she watched Synnamon and Conner and their baby?

Don't be ridiculous, she told herself. Ridge could be good company. He was an eloquent storyteller, an amusing companion, a worthy opponent in argument. Certainly he was more fun than the average guest at this cocktail party.

But it wasn't as if she missed him overwhelmingly, or felt restless when he wasn't around...

Oh, don't you, my girl? She was starting to recognize that quiet little voice, and it annoyed her to know that it was speaking truths she'd rather not face. *You feel more alive when you're squabbling with him than any other time. You miss him, all right. Maybe you even want him...*

Reluctantly, she focused her gaze on a hand waving before her eyes. "Hello?" Alan Davis said. "Morea, are you okay?"

She blinked. "Sure. Hi, Alan."

"I thought you were never going to get here. Don't you have a drink yet? I don't know what the deal is, but George's even serving champagne tonight. With strawberries, yet."

"All right." She'd have agreed to anything that would take Alan away from her side for a couple of minutes and give her a chance to deal with the sudden confusion which had swept over her. Not that she wanted to examine her feelings too closely...

Not here, she thought in something close to panic, *and not now*. She'd have to think it all through later, when there was time and leisure—whether she wanted to or not. But right now she just needed a moment to catch her breath.

Alan had started toward the bar, but he took only a couple of steps before turning back to Morea. "Look at that," he said. "I wonder why he's here."

Morea glanced up automatically to see who he meant. The crowd had parted for a moment, and she could see almost to the front door.

Ridge was standing in the archway between living room and foyer, a champagne glass already in his hand. As if he'd felt her presence, he turned his head, and his gaze locked with hers.

Her first reaction was delight, a tidal wave of happiness. Then, as suddenly as a wave retreated from the shore, the pleasure was gone, to be replaced by a surge of something close to despair. Abruptly, Morea faced a truth that was not only frightening but oddly familiar— as if deep inside some part of her had always known it, but been unwilling to look.

She respected Ridge all right, and liked him—but those things didn't begin to describe how she really felt about him. She didn't simply miss him when he wasn't around. And it wasn't a matter of desire, either—or at least, it wasn't only that.

Somehow, despite professionalism, despite their many disagreements, despite her best intentions, she'd fallen in love with Ridge Coltrain.

CHAPTER NINE

AT FIRST, Morea tried to tell herself that the sudden surge of gladness she'd felt at the mere sight of Ridge was only because company cocktail parties were usually so dull, and he represented a delightful break in the routine.

But she wouldn't have gotten far as an attorney if she hadn't learned to accept reality and deal with it instead of blindly holding out for dreams. That long, tough training kicked in now with a vengeance, refusing to allow her to dodge the facts.

Somewhere, in the midst of their arguments, their opposition, their negotiations, rivalry had turned to respect, and then had inched into something more—something that she didn't even want to consider at this moment. Her common sense and objectivity had been knocked for a loop, and only time would help her get her balance back.

But in the middle of a cocktail party, with Ridge just across the room, she didn't have the luxury of meditation. And thinking on her feet in this situation was likely to be a bit more difficult than in any courtroom she'd ever been in. She thought wryly that she'd have given a great deal right now to be able to say, *Your Honor, if we could take a brief recess...*

Ridge didn't look surprised to see her. But of course he wasn't, Morea thought. He'd have expected her to be present. She, on the other hand, wouldn't have dreamed up this scenario in a hundred years—and she'd been too stunned by the revelation of her own feelings to even wonder at first why he was there. Now, as her pulse gradually slowed toward normal, she found herself asking what on earth Ridge Coltrain was doing in George Bradley's living room with a champagne flute in his hand.

She didn't realize she'd spoken the thought aloud until Alan answered. "Maybe he's crashing the party. In this crowd, George will probably never notice him. Though I must admit my first thought was to wonder if you'd invited him."

"*Me*?" Morea's voice was little more than a squeak. "Oh, you must be thinking of that silly scene outside my office yesterday. You obviously don't know Ridge very well, or you'd take everything he says with not just a grain of salt but a whole block." Determined to look casual, she fluttered a hand in Ridge's direction and then turned her back on him to smile up at Alan. Her lips felt like wood, but the effort apparently convinced her partner.

"Well, that's a relief." Alan had apparently forgotten about offering her champagne, because he made no further move to leave her side. "There's Trent Paxton, headed this way. I didn't think he'd miss a chance to see you. You're all he talks about, Morea."

Just what I need, Morea thought. "That'll be a first— a divorce client who's infatuated instead of hating me."

"Morea, who could hate you?" Alan reached around her to shake Trent's hand. "Hi, buddy. How are things going?"

"Just great." Trent's gaze never left Morea. "You don't mind if I ask a question about my divorce, do you? I mean, I know it's a party, but it's a company party, right? You must be planning to talk law. And you can bill me if you want."

Morea tried to stifle her sigh. If answering his question now kept him out of her office for a precious hour next week, it might be worth it. Besides, any inquiry of Trent

Paxton's was almost guaranteed to take her mind off Ridge and her own problems. "Thanks for giving me permission," she said wryly. "Go ahead."

"You're going to do your best to be fair to both sides in my divorce, you said."

Morea suspected that Trent was going to turn out to be a world champion at asking leading questions. "Yes," she said firmly. "Why? Are you still determined to pinch every last cent?"

"Oh, no," Trent assured her. "Alan here explained to me why it's a good idea to give Daisy a little extra, even if I don't owe it to her."

Thanks a lot, Alan, Morea thought wryly. *And no doubt I'll have to spend at least a couple of hours sorting out the misunderstandings you've caused.*

"My question is," Trent went on, "if you're looking after both sides, why do I have to pay two attorneys? What's Daisy's lawyer going to be doing besides gouging me?"

"Believe me," Morea said, "he or she will be busy. And the reason Daisy should have a lawyer of her own is that any agreement she makes without independent legal advice won't stand up for a minute in court."

Trent looked thoughtful. "So she could agree to something, and then as soon as she feels unhappy about anything she can sue me all over again?"

"Exactly—because the judge would wonder whether she was unfairly pressured into making that agreement."

Trent was frowning.

"Look at Daisy's attorney as if he were car insurance," Morea said. "It's a nuisance to pay, and most of the time you get nothing in return for your money—but it's a necessary expense. And if you do get into an accident, you'll be happy you forked over the premium."

"Oh, I see." Trent winked. "Then maybe you can

recommend somebody. You know—someone who'll fill the position and let you take care of all the details."

"Even if I knew the kind of putz you're talking about," Morea said icily, "I wouldn't give you a name."

Alan intervened. "Ethically, she can't, Trent."

Morea glared at him. "And you'd better not interfere again," she said under her breath. "I'm having enough problems with this client without your so-called help, Alan."

He looked wounded. "I was only trying—"

"Oh, you lawyers always stick together," Trent said with disgust.

Morea knew Ridge was standing just behind her, even before he spoke. There was a sudden sensitivity along the side of her throat, where his hand had rested last night as he kissed her. The sensation reminded her of the aftereffects of a sunburn—her skin suddenly began to tingle, itch, and feel uncomfortably warm.

"Especially the ones in big practices," Ridge agreed. "It's part of the partnership code."

Morea had never noticed before that his mouth was precisely on a level with her ear, so even the most casual comment, made from a perfectly respectable distance, seemed to be an intimate murmur directly to her. His words seemed to stroke her skin.

"Hi," he said. "Just for curiosity's sake, Morea, when did you realize that you left your briefcase in my office last night?"

In fact, she hadn't noticed at all. How, she wondered, had she managed not to notice that it was missing? Generally, that leather case was as closely attached to her as if with an umbilical cord.

"It entertained me all afternoon," Ridge went on.

Morea bristled.

Before she could speak, Ridge seemed to anticipate

her challenge. "Not the contents, you understand, just the fact that you'd walked off and left it, and that you didn't return to retrieve it. I concluded that you didn't quite dare come back."

"Not at all," she said coolly. "In fact, I still hadn't noticed it was missing." *That should squelch him*, she thought. The idea of suggesting that she didn't dare set foot in his office, as if something wild would necessarily happen...

She fought down the warmth which threatened to flood her face at the mere memory of that big chair of his flat on its back in the middle of his office, cradling the two of them.

"Oh, I can see how you wouldn't miss it today," Ridge mused. "It's Saturday, after all, and even TBC can't expect you to work around the clock on weekends, too. What puzzles me is how you managed to get home last night without realizing it was gone... Of course, you did have other things on your mind at the time. Alan," he added mildly, "you look a bit tense. Has it been a tough week?"

Alan didn't look tense, Morea thought. He looked astounded. She glared at Ridge. "I need to talk to you. Privately."

"But I haven't even met everyone," he protested. "Isn't that the reason for a cocktail party in the first place? To get acquainted with new people?"

Morea smothered the growl she'd have liked to utter, and as perfunctorily as possible made the introductions.

Ridge shook hands. "Paxton," he said gently. "Paxton. The name sounds familiar somehow..."

"Excuse us, please." Morea tucked her hand under Ridge's elbow and tried to urge him away. She could feel the hard warmth of his muscles even through the tailored sleeve of his jacket. She felt a bit like a tugboat

trying to move a reluctant ocean liner; unless the liner
wanted to move, she couldn't do much but tread water.

He hesitated for only another moment, though, before
he laid his hand atop hers, smiled down at her, and said,
"How private a space do we need, my dear?"

Morea gritted her teeth and tried not to see the suspicion in Alan's face. She glanced around the room.
"That little alcove by the fireplace should do it."

Ridge eased their passage across the room with a
touch on a shoulder, a pat on the back, an easy smile
here and there, as if he were a politician working the
crowd. Finally they reached the alcove, and he leaned
against a built-in bookcase and looked down at Morea,
one eyebrow lifted. "If this is about your briefcase," he
began, "Scouts' honor—I didn't look inside."

"You'd better not have. There's such a thing as professional ethics, Coltrain."

"And I abided by the rules. Besides, it was locked."
She almost shrieked. "You actually checked?"

"Well, I had to be certain it was yours."

"It has my initials on it, Ridge. Or do so many women
leave personal possessions in your office that you can't
keep the names straight?"

He nodded earnestly. "That's exactly it. I suppose
they do it so they have a good excuse for coming back
to see me again. You know, I'm starting to be worried
about you, Morea. This is the second time in just a few
days that you've lost track of your briefcase."

It took Morea a moment to remember the previous
time—the night he and her father had occupied her home
office. "Don't waste your time worrying. It only happens when I'm around you."

"My point precisely," Ridge mused. "I think there's
something Freudian about it, myself. The briefcase is out
in my car."

"That's very kind of you."

"I'd go get it, but I hate to leave the party, especially when it means leaving *you*," he went on earnestly. "But if you'd like to reclaim it at the end of the evening—"

Morea could just see herself leaving the party with him—saying goodnight as a twosome to George Bradley and his wife, walking out to Ridge's convertible together... By Monday morning, the whole firm would have concluded he'd moved into her apartment.

She suppressed a shiver. "I'll get it tomorrow. At least that way I can tell myself there's some reason to go to tea with your mother." Instantly she regretted the catty note in her voice; she was actually almost looking forward to tea—or at least to seeing Rowena again.

"Then perhaps it was something about Mr. Paxton that you wanted to tell me," Ridge speculated. "Or—I've got it—perhaps it concerns Mrs. Paxton?"

"*No.*" Morea's voice was more forceful than she'd planned. "I want to talk to you about the Madison case, and why on earth you think it might be necessary to give it up. I can't see any reason for it."

"Is that a fact?" Ridge's voice was absolutely casual, as if the subject didn't interest him at all.

Morea was startled. She'd expected him to want an explanation of her reasoning, at least. She wouldn't even have been surprised if he'd argued the point. What she wasn't prepared for was a complete lack of concern.

Ridge added, "Of course, I'd already reached the same conclusion. I think I said as much last night."

But then you kissed me and my world turned upside down. Morea almost said it aloud, and she had to bite her tongue hard to keep the words from slipping out.

She felt as if the floor had started to rock under her feet. *My world...* That was the key phrase, of course. Last night her feelings for Ridge had still been buried, hidden deep in her subconscious. But they'd been no less real than they were now, and she had reacted accordingly. She'd even allowed herself to wonder if he might feel the same sort of overwhelming attraction for her that she felt for him. It had been no more than a fleeting thought, of course, and she'd instantly argued herself out of pursuing it. Or at least she'd tried, and convinced herself that she had succeeded.

But Ridge's world had apparently not been changed at all by that kiss—not, at least, in any way which mattered. It had been only her imagination, her desires, which had painted him as shaken by the experience as she had been. In fact, though he'd talked a whole lot of nonsense last night about appearances, he hadn't really said much of anything. And overall, his behavior had been just one more example of his unparalleled skill at keeping her off balance.

"But of course I'd be interested in hearing your reasons," he added gently.

Morea swallowed hard. *Get yourself out of this one, Landon*, she ordered, *and fast*. "I was simply trying to put your mind at ease," she said stiffly. "There's nothing going on which creates an ethical problem for either of us, or for Kathy and Bill, either."

"How sweet of you," Ridge murmured. "Going out of your way to avoid rocking the boat for them."

Morea wanted to hit him. "The only way a problem might arise is if one of them is uncomfortable with the situation. If they are, it will be for purely imaginary reasons, of course—but one has to abide by the client's wishes."

"Of course," Ridge murmured.

"And if it comes to that, I'll be the one to excuse myself. I'll simply tell Kathy I have to turn her case over to someone else."

"Why would you do that, Morea?" His voice was cool, as if he were asking only to be polite.

"Because you need the fee worse than I do," Morea snapped.

"But your replacement can't even be within the firm, or it's still a conflict of interest. And you'd have to explain the whole thing to your senior partners." Ridge shook his head. "Not an easy thing to do. I, on the other hand, only have to face myself in the mirror in the morning."

She told herself it was only a cliché, a standard phrase rendered meaningless by careless overuse. But she couldn't keep herself from creating the picture in her mind of Ridge, reflected in a steamy bathroom mirror. Muscular arms, bare chest, pajamas riding low on a narrow waist, hair soft and tousled, eyelids heavy, body warm and still sleep-scented...

She wasn't sure how she knew that first thing in the morning he'd be lazy and relaxed, with only the bristly stubble of his beard forming a counterpoint to his body's ease. But she knew it as clearly as she knew Colorado's divorce law.

Ridge's voice was soft. "You'll be glad when this case is over, won't you?"

"Of course I will." Her answer was fast and emphatic, and instantly Morea thought better of it. "I'm always pleased when a case is completed." *But maybe not this time*, she thought, with painful honesty. *Because as long as the case goes on, I can continue to see him. Once it's over...*

There was, of course, her father's case. But Ridge's part in that would soon be finished, too, and then there would be nothing.

"I thought that was what you meant. If that's all, Morea, I should probably search out Mr. Bradley and introduce myself."

Morea knew she should simply nod and let him go. But despite her best intentions she heard herself ask,

"Introduce yourself? Then Alan's wrong and you're not gate-crashing. What are you doing here anyway?"

Ridge shrugged. "Darned if I know. I got an invitation, and I hardly thought it would be polite to call up someone like George Bradley and ask why he'd sent it."

"No doubt the invitation got to you by mistake," Morea said crisply. "You know how these things go."

"Are you implying that anyone at Taylor Bradley Cummings—much less a senior partner—could make a careless mistake? Morea, my treasure, your lack of loyalty is shocking." But the gleam she was used to seeing in his eyes was absent, and his tone seemed a bit abstracted, the endearment oddly flat.

She hadn't yet found an answer when she heard George Bradley's booming voice right behind her. "I see you found our special guest, Morea. But of course— you two already know each other, don't you?"

Too well, Morea wanted to say. But her newfound sensitivity warned that there could be more than one interpretation of that smart remark. Odd, she thought. Yesterday she'd have said it without a qualm, and meant only that their courtroom encounters hadn't always been pleasant. Today...

"In fact," George Bradley went on, "it's entirely due to you that he's here tonight, Morea."

"Me?" She must have looked as stunned as she felt, for she saw a reluctant smile tug at the corner of Ridge's mouth—as if despite himself he was too amused not to react.

"Really?" he murmured. "You're too modest, Morea. Accusing me of breaking into a party, when you're the one who arranged for my invitation!"

"I didn't." The protest sprang automatically to her lips.

"But it was you who brought Ridge to my attention," George explained. "You see, it was only when I started looking for defamation specialists for you that I realized Ridge's office was right downstairs. How we all could have missed that..."

Morea was thoroughly confused. "But I don't see—"

"You didn't know he's one of the best defamation attorneys in the western half of the country?"

Ridge said, "Oh, I wouldn't go that far, Mr. Bradley."

"Now don't be modest, my boy. It's not becoming." He turned to Morea. "This is the man who won the Carey case out in Los Angeles. You know, the one I told you about."

Morea's eyes narrowed. "You said you practiced in Phoenix." She was practically gritting her teeth.

Ridge shrugged. "I did. I also told you it was too hot for my taste there in the summertime, so if a case came along somewhere else, of course I jumped at the chance..."

"Right. As if you choose cases based solely on geography."

"Absolutely not," he said crisply. "Sometimes I get manipulated into taking them."

Morea didn't know why she suddenly felt like crying. Of course, this was the third shock she'd had to absorb within a limited time and in front of an unlimited audience.

And what a surprise this one was! He'd been toying with her professionally, as well as personally. He'd known perfectly well she'd been searching for a specialist to take her father's case, but he hadn't bothered to tell her that he had experience in the very field she'd been seeking...

She was just glad she hadn't given herself away by letting him guess how she felt about him. That would have been a final, bitter blow.

George Bradley's voice seemed to come from a distance, almost drowned out by the drone of angry thoughts in Morea's head. "In fact," he said expansively, "I'm going to do my best to persuade him to join the firm. We could use an enthusiastic young man with a special gift for some tough areas of the law—and we're prepared to make a very good offer. So be a good girl and apply yourself to convincing him, all right, Morea?" He patted her on the shoulder, shook Ridge's hand with enthusiasm, and was gone to greet the next small group.

"I wonder what he meant by that," Ridge said thoughtfully. "Being a good girl and applying yourself to convincing me, I mean. It could have quite interesting implications."

Suddenly the lazy good humor was back in his voice, and that fact stirred Morea to fury and to an even deeper pain. If he could so lightheartedly tease her, after everything that had happened...

What a gullible fool she'd been!

"Don't get any ideas," she said curtly. "In the first place, I don't particularly want to convince you, and in the second place, I hardly think convincing would be necessary."

"Oh, no, it's not. But it might be fun nevertheless."

Morea said, with a tinge of bitterness, "So much for all your fine talk about independent practice. Though I'd suggest it would be wise not to sign on too quickly." Her voice felt as brittle as it sounded. "You may as well hold out a while, and get an even better deal."

"What would you suggest I ask for?"

There was a note of humility in his voice, Morea thought. "If George wants you badly enough—and apparently he does—he may even offer you a full partnership."

"Do you think so?" Ridge mused. "I seem to remember saying I thought we'd be great partners, Morea."

Morea had to swallow hard before she could manage just the right touch of wryness. "Oh, yes," she said. "In fact, I can hardly wait."

By the time Morea could make her excuses and go home, her nerves felt like bridge cables—drawn tight and humming with tension. And she'd actually thought, when she first glimpsed him across the room, that Ridge's presence might make the party more enjoyable!

She tried to convince herself that working with him would be less stressful than opposing him. With him in the same partnership, she wouldn't have to be trying to outthink him in every encounter.

At least, she thought wryly, that would be true on a professional level. She could save her wary watchfulness in order to guard her emotional well-being every time she ran into him in the executive dining room, or the hallway, or at the coffee machine...

Or perhaps she would see even less of him than she did now. Taylor Bradley Cummings wouldn't offer him the earth on a silver platter—as George Bradley had made so apparent tonight they were willing to do—to mess around with average cases. He'd be taking on the high-profile ones, the risky ones. He'd be in charge of his own team, no doubt—a team Morea would almost never encounter. He'd be traveling...

She didn't know which was worse. Seeing him, or not seeing him. Cooperating with him, working against him, or not encountering him at all.

All she knew was that no matter what he thought about her, she cared for him—and she always would. That blinding revelation hadn't been her imagination.

She only wished it had been.

Without her briefcase, Morea couldn't even distract herself with work. The hours dragged, and finally, early on

Sunday afternoon, she abandoned her apartment with the intention of simply driving around Denver until time for Rowena's tea.

Instead she found herself in the hospital, standing outside the nursery window. The infinitesimal crib which had held Synnamon's baby was empty, so Morea turned down the hall toward her friend's room and tapped on the door. "Is the little princess receiving visitors?" she asked.

Synnamon, already dressed in street clothes, was bundling the baby into a blanket. "You're just in time to hold her while I finish doing my hair."

"You're going home already?"

Synnamon nodded. "As soon as Conner gets here."

Before Morea could consider whether she wanted to hold the baby, the warm, wriggly bundle was in her arms. She cradled the infant awkwardly. "Am I doing this right?"

Synnamon considered. "You look like a natural."

"Then why do I feel so clumsy? Every muscle in my back aches already."

"That's not the baby's weight you feel, it's the responsibility." Synnamon vanished into the bathroom. "Guess who showed up to see me this morning," she called.

The least likely person Morea could think of was Ridge—and she knew better than to utter his name. Synnamon would think she had nothing else on her mind.

Which you don't, Morea reminded herself. *Let's be honest about that much, at least.*

She looked down at the warm bundle in her arms, and was startled to see the baby staring at her with the same curiosity. The miniature forehead wrinkled in puzzlement, then relaxed as the baby, apparently reassured, yawned and snuggled closer. Morea's heart twisted.

Synnamon leaned around the edge of the door. "Are you two doing all right?"

"Fine. But I always thought being wrapped around someone's finger was just an expression—till now. I actually felt it happen."

Synnamon laughed. "I should have warned you. Holding a baby is not only dangerous to your emotional health but to your career goals. It seems to jump-start the biological clock somehow."

"Gee, thanks. Just what I need." She shifted the baby slightly and asked, trying to sound casual, "So who came to see you this morning?"

"Daisy Paxton. Can you believe it? I haven't seen the woman in weeks, but she turns up here. Wanting, of all things, a suggestion for a divorce attorney. I suggested she call Ridge—"

Every muscle in Morea's body tensed. "You didn't!"

The baby's eyes opened abruptly and her face wrinkled up as if she was about to cry. Feeling incredibly inept, Morea tried to soothe her.

"Why not?" Synnamon asked. "You said there was nothing going on between you."

"There isn't."

"So why don't you want him to represent Daisy Paxton?"

"It isn't that." With relief, she remembered the offer Ridge had received from George Bradley last night. "He's joining TBC, so he can't work the opposing side of a case we've already taken on."

"I see. Well, there's still no problem, right?" Synnamon twisted her hair up into a neat roll and clipped it at her crown. She tucked her brush into the bag which lay on her bed. "How do you feel about having Ridge in the same practice?"

"Neutral." Morea saw the doubt in Synnamon's eyes

and added defensively, "How should I feel? He'll be my partner, for heaven's sake."

"It would be the first time you ever felt neutral about Ridge Coltrain."

"That's true," Morea said, trying to sound as if the idea hadn't occurred to her. "He's not a neutral sort of person."

"And since you never date your partners..."

"Believe me," Morea said flatly, "keeping that resolution will not be a problem."

Not, she thought, *that I wouldn't like it to be...*

Ridge was nowhere in evidence when Morea arrived at the Coltrain house for tea. But Rowena was in the kitchen, scooping tiny tea cakes off a baking pan onto a glass tray. She looked slightly harried, but the moment Morea came in, her face relaxed. "Hello, dear. I'm so glad to see you."

Morea's conscience gave a guilty little twitch before she reminded herself that it hadn't been her idea to lie to Rowena. Let Ridge sort it all out. But she had to admit she would miss having the opportunity to know Rowena better. Funny that after only one evening together, she knew that they could have been friends.

Morea kept her voice light. "Same here. Can I help? I'm not wonderful in a kitchen, but I can boil water."

"Good—because I'm not sure I can today. I've already burned two pans of tea cakes."

Morea filled the teakettle. "Where's Ridge, anyway? It's his party, so he's the one who ought to be in charge of snacks. Surely he isn't working today?"

"He's trying to round up the squirrels."

"Well, that's a good job for him."

"He doesn't often work weekends, anyway," Rowena said.

"That'll change now that he's joining Taylor Bradley

Cummings." She stole a glance at Rowena. "You don't look surprised. Did you already know that?"

"No—but then he never talks to me about his cases or his profession. He's never even breathed a word of regret about leaving his practice in Phoenix when I got sick... There's the doorbell. It must be your parents, Morea. Would you go and greet them?"

Ridge had heard the bell, too, and had already opened the door when Morea reached the front hall. He kissed Meredith's cheek and held out his hand to Charles, who shook it firmly as he came in.

Meredith Landon was looking great, Morea thought, her silver hair perfectly styled and her flowery summer dress taking ten years off her age. Charles looked better, too, she could see at a glance. She hadn't seen him since the night he and Ridge had had their heart-to-heart, but he seemed more relaxed, even at ease, as he greeted the younger man. As if he hadn't a care or a secret in the world.

Morea had been worried, of course—but she didn't realize how heavy a weight that concern had been until it dropped off her shoulders now. How glad she was that it wouldn't be necessary to find yet another attorney to represent him! He was obviously comfortable with Ridge. Morea had always felt that the client's confidence, along with the attorney's experience, were the most important factors in creating a successful case. With Ridge, Charles was fortunate enough to have both.

She still didn't entirely understand why Ridge hadn't told her of his previous experience, but nevertheless some of the resentment she'd felt last night when George Bradley dropped his bombshell began to dissipate. The important thing was that Charles get the best advice—the rest hardly mattered.

Rowena came up behind her, a plate of tea cakes in each hand, and led the way to the sunporch. "You two

go and get the tea while the rest of us introduce ourselves," she directed Ridge and Morea. "I left the pot
brewing in the kitchen."

Obediently, Morea retraced her steps, finding the tray
already set up. She checked the tea and decided it needed
to steep for another minute or two.

Ridge was extraordinarily quiet, she thought. The silence made her nervous, but she didn't quite know how
to break it. No casual quips came to mind, and she certainly didn't want to sound serious.

She watched him from the corner of her eye. He was
informally dressed, his polo shirt open at the throat, the
short sleeves leaving his arms bare. He exuded power,
as always, though he'd seemed to turn the wattage down
today. But there was something different about him, she
thought. A certain wariness, perhaps—even more than
she'd picked up last night at George Bradley's party.

"Do you think you could manage to say hello?"
Ridge asked.

I could ask the same question, Morea thought. But
that would only let him know that she'd noticed how
little they suddenly had to say to each other. "Sorry. I
was hardly paying attention. But I couldn't help but see
how pleased my father was to see you—the two of you
are shaping up to be best friends."

"We played tennis again this morning."

"Well, Daddy's no doubt going to be very disappointed when we stop role-playing—though I suppose
you could still be tennis buddies no matter what. As long
as you're staying on his case..." She paused. "You are,
aren't you?"

"What's this, Morea? A change of heart? Don't
worry, I've promised Charles I'll follow through."

"Well, that's good. Now that you've accomplished
the main purpose, though, are you planning to tell him
that you and I aren't a serious item, or shall I? And

when?'' She scooped the tea ball out of the pot and set it aside. ''For your mother's sake, perhaps right now—''

''I wasn't planning to tell him anything at all,'' Ridge said quietly.

''Very funny. What are you really—''

Before she could finish, Ridge had picked up the tray and carried it off down the hall, leaving her to follow helplessly.

From the sunporch, she could hear voices—mostly Meredith's soft soprano mixing with Rowena's twangier alto. But as Morea stepped through the doorway, Charles cleared his throat and said, in the tone she'd heard before only in a lecture hall, ''I've taught for thirty-two years, Rowena, one place and another. But I'm all finished with that now. I'm retiring, effective immediately. My letter is written, and I'll be putting it in the mail tomorrow morning.''

Each word hit Morea with the force of a hammer blow. Her gaze flashed automatically to Ridge. How was he reacting to this news? Should she reach for the tray, to help steady it?—as if she could, shaking the way she was!

But Ridge's fingers didn't even tremble. *He's got a lot better self-control than I do*, she thought with reluctant admiration as he set the tray down beside his mother's chair. But then Charles wasn't his father, just his client—and heaven knew clients sometimes acted in bizarre and unpredictable ways.

From behind her father's back, Morea beckoned to Ridge, and he slowly worked his way across the sunporch to her.

''What are you going to do?'' she asked under her breath. He didn't answer, and she went on urgently, ''You have to stop him, Ridge. You can't let him do this. He has to fight.''

Ridge sighed. "The trouble is, Morea, I agree with him."

She stared at him, too upset even to speak.

"In fact," he went on gently, "he's acting on my advice."

CHAPTER TEN

MOREA stared at him. It simply wasn't possible that she was hearing him correctly. *Ridge had advised her father to resign?*

Charles Landon reached for his wife's hand. "Meredith knows how long I've been wanting to devote myself to my new book. And I'll be able to fit in a lot more tennis, too—right, son?"

Son? Morea thought woodenly. Ridge looked a bit uncomfortable about that—as well he ought to, she told herself almost viciously. *He'd actually suggested that Charles resign?*

Charles went on, "And time and money for travel with my wife, as well."

Morea turned on Ridge. "I said I'd pick up the bill for this. So if you gave my father this incredible advice because you didn't think he has enough money to pay your fees—"

"Do you think I'd base my advice on whether I'm likely to get paid?"

She heard the edge in Ridge's voice and knew that she had gone just a little too far. But right now she didn't care. *He'd* gone too far, too—dishing out life-changing advice and not even warning her.

She raised her voice. "If you'll excuse us..."

Rowena looked surprised; Meredith seemed a bit worried. Morea wasn't surprised.

Charles grinned. "Run along, kids. No need for you to sit here while the old folks get acquainted, when you could be having fun."

Fun, Morea thought, was a long way from what she

had in mind. She led the way to the kitchen and turned on Ridge, arms folded across her chest, chin up. "How long has this been going on?"

Ridge leaned against the sink. "He told me that night at your apartment why he wanted to resign and have it over with."

She gasped. "And you didn't tell me? You let me think you'd convinced him to fight?"

"Morea, just because he told me he still wanted to resign doesn't mean I agreed that he should. And I want to point out, by the way, that he's not resigning, he's retiring—and there's a whole world of difference."

"Like what?" Morea asked irritably.

"Full pension, continued benefits, status as a professor emeritus—things like that."

Morea shook her head. "Little stuff."

"Not so little when you think about where a straight resignation would have left him—and your mother."

"But compared to the vindication he should have... Dammit, Ridge, you practically told me you were doing what I'd asked, and instead you were working behind my back to do precisely the opposite!"

Ridge said quietly, "Charles is my client, Morea. You're not."

The simple statement stopped Morea cold. It was true; she of all people knew that an attorney owed his loyalty only to his client, no matter who else was involved. The fact that she'd offered to foot the costs gave her no standing. But she'd counted on Ridge needing her help, wanting her advice.

But he'd turned his back on her. She wasn't his client, and he'd declined to make her his colleague.

So what am I to you, Ridge? The question echoed through her head so loudly that for a moment she was afraid she'd said it aloud. Afraid, because she already knew the answer, and she didn't want to hear him say it.

She meant absolutely nothing to him. That much was painfully obvious; if she'd mattered to him at all, he would have explained—or at least warned her.

He owed her that much—but the fact that he didn't seem to see it the same way Morea did only emphasized the gulf between the way she felt about him, and the feelings he didn't possess for her.

She couldn't look at him anymore. "I suppose next you'll try to convince me that if I was representing your mother you wouldn't want a full report."

"I wouldn't," Ridge said. "Because I trust you."

Fury spurted through Morea's veins, hot as molten lava. "Damn you, Ridge Coltrain, that's an absolutely vile thing to say!"

"That I trust you? Why should you take that as an insult, unless it reminds you that you don't trust me? And as long as we're talking of trust, Morea, about this accusation of yours that I based my advice on how much money Charles has—"

Morea hesitated, then said, almost grudgingly, "I didn't mean it that way, exactly."

"What a gracious apology!"

"Oh, I see the world's greatest attorney gets sarcastic on occasion! Ridge, I told you that fighting this case wasn't a matter of money. Didn't I make it perfectly clear that I'd pay for this, no matter what it costs?"

"You said you'd pick up the financial expenditures, yes. But who pays the rest of the bill?"

Morea frowned. "What do you mean?"

"The emotional drain, the stress, the wear and tear of a long battle. Who pays for that, Morea?" He answered the question. "Charles and Meredith—that's who."

"But it's the right thing to do. When there's been an injustice like this, there's no option but to fight."

"Do you honestly believe that nothing but the principle matters? Have you been so indoctrinated at Taylor Bradley Cummings that you really think there is no battle which should be left unfought, no circumstance in which human cost outweighs the principle?"

She was silent for a moment.

"I've negotiated a deal with the university, Morea. Instead of resigning in disgrace, your father is retiring, with full honors and only a couple of years earlier than he'd have to leave his post anyway. No charges will be filed, no legal action taken. He maintains not only his reputation but the practical things like insurance benefits—"

"But he loses his self-respect," Morea said bitterly.

"He doesn't feel that way about it. He's never wanted to fight this, he just didn't know there was another option besides resigning or battling it out. And I became convinced, as I investigated and as I talked to him, that this is the best course of action for Charles."

"But he's innocent, Ridge!"

"It would be a long hard fight to prove it, and unless we could establish his innocence beyond any hint of doubt, the shadow will always lie across his reputation."

"That's my point exactly. He's shadowed now. Unless he fights—"

"But he isn't, Morea. Not really. The university won't pursue the matter. Neither will the student. By retiring now, he's made an end of it—but if we were to fight, it would be on every front page in Colorado. That publicity is what would destroy his reputation, and even if we ultimately won, the stain would always be there. The doubts would persist."

Morea shook her head, more in sadness and defeat than disagreement.

"And what do we have to gain from that battle?" Ridge went on. "Two more years of employment, that's all. Uneasy and uncomfortable years, if he's had to force the issue.''

"How can you be certain the student won't sue? If she does, the fact that Daddy resigned will tend to make him look guilty.''

"On the advice of her attorney, after I spent hours talking to him, she's signed an agreement promising she won't. It wouldn't be good for her career to be caught up in that kind of publicity, either, you know.''

"The last thing I'm worried about is her career.''

"I'm not surprised about that,'' Ridge said dryly. "It didn't concern me a great deal, either—not nearly as much as the matter of your father's health and his stamina for a long fight. He's not a young man, Morea, and he could have this mess hanging over his head for months—maybe even years—with no certainty of a resolution in his favor. With this agreement, he can have what he wants. He can be at peace, to write his books and putter in his garden.''

"And play tennis,'' Morea said bitterly, "with his newfound best buddy.''

She half-expected Ridge to defend himself, but he didn't. Instead, he said quietly, "You're the one who convinced him that it wasn't worth the fight, Morea.''

"I? I've never even talked to him about this whole thing! You can't possibly blame me for his reluctance.''

"The final blow was when you discovered the student's record was so squeaky clean she looks like St. Theresa.''

"Thanks a bunch,'' Morea said. "I'm sure you gave me full credit for that little discovery! You know, Ridge, I can't help but wonder what George Bradley will think of your reluctance to get into a fight. It doesn't sound much like the kind of attorney he seemed to think you were.''

"What he thinks doesn't matter. I'm not going to join TBC."

Morea frowned. "You're not? But you said—"

"You're the one who said I was," Ridge pointed out.

"You certainly didn't deny it. And you'd be an idiot not to. An offer like that doesn't come around regularly, you know."

"Then I'm an idiot."

"Astounding!" Morea snapped. "At last, we've found *something* we agree on!"

Morea's father called her the next morning while she was still dressing. "I'm downstairs in the concierge's office," he said. "I'll take you out for breakfast if you have time."

"Of course, Daddy. Or would you like to come up?"

"No. You can't talk if you're cooking. Let's go around the corner to that little restaurant."

Morea finished brushing her hair, leaving it loose around her shoulders rather than taking the time to pin it up, and put on a red linen jacket, a sharp contrast to her black skirt and crisp white blouse.

Charles was pacing the lobby when she stepped out of the elevator, and his smile didn't quite reach his eyes. "Pretty," he said, with a gesture at her suit. But Morea wasn't certain he'd really seen it—or her.

As soon as they were seated and the waitress had poured their coffee, Charles said abruptly, "Your mother confessed that she'd told you all about the trouble."

He didn't sound upset about the fact, but Morea was cautious nevertheless. "She needed someone to confide in."

He nodded. "I know. I didn't realize at first how much the whole thing was affecting her, as well as me. I know I should have told you, Morea."

Morea stirred her coffee. "I wish you had, Daddy."

"I certainly wasn't trying to keep it from you forever. And it's not that I didn't trust you to back me up. But I didn't need advice, I needed time to think."

"And you felt I'd jump in and tell you what to do." She wasn't asking a question; she was admitting, to herself as well as to him, that she'd have done precisely that.

Charles nodded. "Guess I underestimated you, right? Thanks for letting me work it out in my own way, in my own time—and for not pressuring me to take the legal route."

The lump of guilt in Morea's throat was far too big to swallow. She'd applied all the pressure she could bring to bear; she'd just done it in a different form than he'd expected.

"And also for understanding why I just couldn't talk to you about it until now."

"You couldn't tell me, but you could talk to Ridge." She tried, without much success, to keep the note of bitterness out of her voice.

Charles shrugged. "He's not so close. Not so—important, somehow, as you are." He added, hastily, "It's not that I don't like him, Morea, because I do. I'll be very happy to have him as part of the family."

"Well, don't hire the caterers and the dance band just yet, Daddy." The waitress set a plate in front of her. Morea didn't even remember what she'd ordered until she looked down at a mass of scrambled eggs. Then she wondered why she'd bothered. Had she actually thought she might be able to eat?

Charles picked up his fork. "Ridge suggested I talk to you before I actually mail the letter. I'm not sure why. Something about wanting you to understand that I'd thought this thing all the way through, not just jumped into a decision."

Suddenly Morea felt she couldn't bear hearing it all

again. "He told me all the reasons, and I still don't agree. But I know it's your decision, Daddy, and no one else can make it."

Charles reached across the table to take her hand. "Thank you, darling, for acting like a daughter and not a lawyer."

Morea wished she knew whether or not she should take that as a compliment.

Morea had never before seen her secretary so startled that she'd completely lost her poise, but on Friday afternoon—when she came into Morea's office to announce that Kathy and Bill Madison had arrived for their appointment—Cindy was almost breathless with shock.

"Not only did they come in together," she said, "but they're sitting in the waiting room holding hands!"

"Oh—did I forget to warn you about that?"

"You mean you knew it?" Cindy shook her head. "What's going on around here, anyway? Shall I show them into the conference room, or just suggest a hotel?"

It was the first time all week that Morea had seen any humor in anything, and once started, she laughed until tears were flowing down her cheeks—tears of enjoyment, of stress, of anger, of frustration, of near-hysteria, all mixed into a salty stew.

Cindy watched her in consternation. "It wasn't *that* funny," she suggested finally.

"No," Morea agreed, gasping for breath and calmness, "it wasn't. Don't worry, I'm all right. Really." She reached for a tissue and a hand mirror and dried her tears, trying to blot around her eyes in order to preserve her mascara. Finally, however, she gave it up as impossible and reached for her makeup bag. She didn't dare walk into a settlement conference displaying the obvious marks of tears—even though they'd been mostly ones of humor.

"And Ridge has been here for a few minutes, too," Cindy went on. "He told me not to bother you till the Madisons came."

Morea swore under her breath and then told herself to think positive; with any luck, this would be the last time she'd be late for a conference with Ridge—if only because it was likely to be the last conference.

And, she told herself briskly, there was no sense at all in feeling sad about that. Continued encounters meant only continued pain.

She patched up the damage to her makeup in record time; Cindy was still pouring Ridge's coffee when Morea came into the conference room. On the far side of the oval table, the Madisons sat side by side. That phenomenon alone would have stopped Morea in her tracks if she'd come upon it without warning; it was the first time she'd ever seen them assume anything but an adversarial, across-the-table position.

"I gather the question of who gets the candlesticks has been satisfactorily resolved?" she said.

Kathy's eyes widened. "How'd you know that?"

"I saw..." Morea thought better of commenting about the scene at the Pinnacle. Why ask for questions about what she'd been doing there, and who she'd been with? "...that you're holding hands," she finished, a bit lamely.

She hadn't even looked at Ridge, but she could feel the flicker of amusement which raced through him and was just as quickly quenched. It was frightening, she thought, to realize how closely attuned she'd become to his moods. As she pulled out the chair next to his, she could feel an actual coolness in the air around him.

And just what, she thought irritably, did Ridge have to feel chilly about? She was the one with cause to be annoyed. She no longer resented the advice he'd given her father; she still thought he'd been wrong, but she could respect an honest difference of opinion, and the final decision always belonged to the client. It wouldn't be fair to hold Ridge entirely responsible for Charles' reluctance to fight.

What she couldn't pass over was the fact that he hadn't shared his advice, his thinking process, with her. He could have warned her of the direction the discussion was taking. He could even have asked her opinion. But he hadn't.

She knew why, of course. *Because you don't matter, and so it never occurred to him.*

She wouldn't forget that lapse. It was difficult enough to maintain her balance, simply knowing how unimportant she was to him. But if she buried that memory, she might once more look at Ridge as she had the night of George Bradley's cocktail party, when the truth of her love had struck her like a lightning bolt. And then she would be lost.

Even now—sitting two feet from him, not looking at him, protected by the armored shell she'd assumed to defend herself from his appeal—she was horribly aware of Ridge. The scent of his aftershave tugged at her senses. The tips of her fingers tingled with the desire to smooth the hair at the nape of his neck.

No, she thought. She wouldn't—she didn't dare—forget that he hadn't bothered to explain. That he hadn't seen any reason to.

"We had a good talk," Kathy said.

Morea had to drag her attention back to the conference room and force herself to focus on her client's face. Kathy, she thought, looked self-conscious and perhaps just a little ashamed of herself.

Kathy looked down at the table. "I guess we should have done it long ago. Before we caused all this trouble."

"We both had a lot of misperceptions," Bill said. "I

thought Kathy wanted the divorce no matter what, so there was no sense in talking.''

Kathy squeezed his hand. "And I thought Bill had made up his mind. We've already had two sessions with a counselor this week, and we know we've got a long way to go. But we're both willing to try.''

"Congratulations," Morea said. "And the best of luck.''

"Unfortunately," Ridge put in, "there are still a few details to mop up before you can just walk away. I hate to sound like Scrooge, but for instance, I'd like to know if we're putting this action on hold or calling it off altogether. It makes a difference in how we handle the paperwork.''

The final details were quickly settled, and within half an hour the Madisons were gone, still hand in hand. Morea leaned back in her chair, contemplating the things yet to be done.

"I have to admit I wish they'd tried talking before we went to all this work," Ridge said. There was a tart note in his voice.

And all this togetherness. Just look at the trouble it led to. Was she actually reading his mind, Morea wondered, or only assuming that must be what he was thinking?

"I distinctly remember suggesting counseling," she pointed out, "to Kathy alone, and to both of them in the first joint session we had. But I suppose even if they'd gone it wouldn't have done any good then." Morea started to gather up her folders. "Well, I'll get the paperwork finished and send copies down to you." She pushed her chair back, but she didn't stand up.

She'd known, of course, that this was the end. But suddenly the fact hit her like a brick: They might never be together like this again.

And I'm glad, she reminded herself. *It hurts to see him. If I don't see him, it will hurt less.*

"You look unhappy," Ridge said quietly. "Have you been crying?"

She'd fixed her mascara, but nothing except time could erase the redness in her eyes. "Oh—yes, as a matter of fact. Cindy told a joke earlier that was so funny I laughed till I cried."

He didn't believe her; Morea could see the doubt in his gaze. But his voice was light. "Maybe I'll ask her to tell me."

"She might," Morea said. "Though it's not your sort of joke. I still have that file, by the way."

Ridge frowned.

"The one on Daddy's student," she went on. "We talked about what was in it, but I never gave it to you." She tried to keep herself from turning pink at the memory of precisely why she'd forgotten to give him the file. She only hoped he'd put the memory of the tipped-over chair in his office farther from his mind that she'd been able to.

"You actually have copies?"

Morea nodded. "The file's been in my briefcase all this time, but I suppose it should be part of your case record."

Ridge shrugged. "I can't see that it matters, now that we've got an agreement."

"Well, you may as well have it anyway. Come into my office."

Her briefcase stood beside her desk; Morea lifted it onto the blotter and automatically adjusted the combination locks till the lid snapped open. The folder was buried, and she had to sort through a stack to find it.

From the corner of her eye, she could see Ridge studying her office. "If you're having second thoughts about turning down George Bradley's offer..." She was talking more to fill the silence than because she thought he might admit it.

"No. I was just thinking about this practice. Insulated, easy—almost too perfect."

Morea pulled the folder out. *Perfect*, she thought. Now why should that single word make her feel jittery?

"For instance," Ridge went on, "what will the senior partners say about the Madison case coming apart?"

Morea didn't even hear him. "*Too perfect*. That's it!"

"What?"

She thumped the folder down in front of him. "She's too perfect. Her record is too good. Nobody can be that squeaky clean."

"Morea, this is called wishful thinking, and somebody should have knocked it out of you during your first semester of law school."

"Read it, Ridge. Just look through that file, and see if you don't agree that it's so spotless it's fishy."

"Your father's already reached a settlement."

"I know. But..." Her voice trailed off. She looked down at the folder and bit her lip. "I'm being foolish, I suppose."

He didn't actually say it, but she knew what he was thinking. That was another uncomfortable side effect of falling in love with him—though in this instance she had to admit there was no talent required to read his mind. She *was* being foolish.

She held out a hand, trying to be casual. "Well, it's been nice opposing you."

He shook it, briefly. "Yes. See you around, Morea."

"Right."

It was no big deal, she told herself. It wasn't as if she was saying goodbye to him forever.

But in a very real sense, she knew she was. Now that she was aware of her feelings, the code of professional ethics said she could never again go up against him in a courtroom. And since he wasn't joining TBC, she could never cooperate with him, either.

Never. She hadn't realized before what a depressing word it could be.

Morea idly stirred her chef's salad, stabbed a cherry tomato and stared at it for a moment, then laid her fork down with a sigh and looked around the room. Taylor Bradley Cummings' executive dining room was almost empty; she'd deliberately waited till most of the lunch crowd was gone before coming in. She'd considered going to the Pinnacle instead, but it held too many memories now; she was no longer comfortable there, because all she could think of was Ridge.

"You've been different lately," Alan Davis said suddenly.

The sound of his voice startled her; she'd actually forgotten he was sitting across the table from her. "Have I?" Morea asked warily. She pushed her plate aside.

"Got a case bothering you?"

"No more than usual. Trent Paxton's coming in this afternoon, so I need to get back to my office."

Alan strolled along beside her down the wide, quiet hall. "You're still going to the bar association banquet this weekend, aren't you?"

Morea had actually managed to forget it. "Do I have a choice?"

"The grapevine says George managed to finagle some honor for Ridge Coltrain. It's part of his campaign to get him into the firm, I suppose. Is he going to join?"

"How should I know?"

"You aren't still seeing him, then?"

"Not since the Madison case got settled."

Alan laughed. "You're getting a reputation, you know. Trent heard about that and asked me in horror if all your clients got back together."

"You can reassure him on that score. Frankly, I'm not so sure Daisy Paxton won't be better off without him." She'd still do her best for Trent, however, even though she'd like to toss him out of her office this afternoon and never see him again.

There were times when the idea of being more independent—of being able to choose or turn down cases without any excuse at all, much less a reason strong enough to persuade the senior partners—was incredibly attractive.

But that wasn't quite the whole truth, she admitted. It wasn't the freedom alone she found so beguiling. And it wasn't a solo practice she envisioned, either. It was a small, intimate double office, with Ridge right next door...

A voice in the back of her brain jeered, *Isn't it time you start living realistically, Morea?*

She said, abruptly, "Do you still want to go to the banquet together, Alan?"

His astonishment was so complete it was almost unflattering. "Yes. Sure." He grinned. "I can't believe it, Morea—we actually have a date."

Almost automatically, she said, "It's not a date." Then she forced herself to smile. "Dates are supposed to be fun, and a bar association banquet hardly fits that description."

Alan pulled open the door of her office suite. "Then we'll have to do something else, another night, to make up for it."

Morea hesitated. She couldn't get over Ridge by sitting at home obsessing; getting out in public, no matter who she was with, would do her good. But it wouldn't be fair to Alan to raise his hopes when she knew she could never be serious about him. "We'll see," she said, and closed the door behind her.

She half-expected Trent to be in the waiting room,

though he'd been habitually late for his appointments. So for a moment, when her gaze focused on the man who was sitting in a deep wing-backed leather chair opposite Cindy's desk, she thought she must be imagining things.

It had been less than two weeks since Ridge had left her office after the Madisons' final appointment, when she'd told herself that not seeing him would hurt less than having to face him. But she'd been wrong. Only now did she realize how hungry she'd been simply for the sight of him.

He looked a bit thinner, she thought. His face seemed more chiseled somehow, as if the underlying muscles had turned to rock, and there was no spark of humor in his eyes. Whatever had brought him here, she thought, he didn't expect to enjoy it.

"May I have a few minutes?" he asked quietly.

"I have a client coming in."

"It won't take long."

"All right. Coffee?"

"No, thanks."

Then he really didn't intend to stay long, Morea knew. For Ridge to turn down Cindy's coffee...

She led the way into her office and pointed to a chair, but Ridge didn't sit down.

Instead, he stood in the precise center of the Oriental rug in front of her desk. "You were right on target about that student."

It took Morea a moment to realize what he'd said. "What do you mean?"

"Her file, her entire record, was perfect," Ridge went on. "I've never seen such glowing recommendations as the ones the professors at her former school had written. Just as a matter of principle, I started calling them up— and as soon as I started asking questions, it was apparent that the people who had written those recommendations were very nervous.''

"Why should they be?"

"That's what I wanted to know, but it was so well buried it took the better part of a week to dig out the facts." He paused. "They were jittery because she'd accused two of her professors of sexual harassment, and her price for staying quiet was those recommendations."

Morea took a deep breath. "This wasn't the first time she'd done it?"

"Exactly. And she learns fast. Last time she demanded references so she could transfer to another school. This time she forced your father to retire, so she didn't have to move on."

Morea groped for her chair and sat down.

"It took some pressure to break her down—she's one very cool customer. But she finally admitted she falsified the charges. I've got her signed statement and an apology from her attorney."

"Then Daddy doesn't have to leave his job after all." Morea's head was spinning. "But since he already has—"

"The university has assured me they'd take him back in a moment."

"Ridge, that's wonderful news!" Tears were stinging her eyelids. "He'll have his career back—"

He held up a hand as if to fend her off. "If he wants it. At the moment, I'm not sure he does. When I called to tell him, he thanked me for letting him know, asked if I'd like to play tennis over the weekend, and excused himself because he was in the middle of an important concept in chapter three."

"He must have been absorbed. It'll no doubt hit him later."

"Well, I'm only telling you so you won't blame me if he stays retired."

Morea said, "I wasn't blaming you. I was trying to thank you."

"You're the one who had the intuition," Ridge said quietly. "I was stupid enough to take things at face value."

"We all do that once in a while." She tried to smile. "Remember? Mine was the Simmons case, when you caught me off guard."

"And you've paid me back for that one," Ridge mused.

Morea's throat tightened. Did he really think she was so petty that she'd brought up the Simmons case in order to revel in revenge?

"Your mother started making noises about a celebration dinner, by the way, for the four of us."

He made it sound like a warning, Morea thought. She forced herself to smile. "Enjoy yourself—you've earned it. I'll make sure I'm too busy to come."

The door of her office opened with such force that it banged against the wall and rebounded, almost hitting Trent Paxton in the nose. Startled, Morea sat up straight in her chair as he rushed in, with Cindy right behind him.

"I have an appointment, dammit," Trent shouted. "You're only a secretary and you have no right to keep me from seeing my attorney!" He brushed Cindy's hand off his arm and appealed to Morea. "Daisy's hired some hotshot called Ridge Coltrain, and Alan says he's dangerous. Now what are we going to do?"

Morea stood up. Her voice was quiet and firm. "You are going back out to Cindy's office, where you will sit down, shut up, and wait your turn."

Trent didn't seem to hear. "Do you know any way to get around him?"

"I don't think you need to worry about that. By the way, in case you don't remember meeting Mr. Coltrain, shall I introduce you again?'' Trent went rigid. Morea took one of his elbows, Cindy took the other, and they ushered him out.

Morea closed the office door gently and leaned against it. She stayed there for a long moment, looking across the room at Ridge.

"So you took Daisy's case," she said finally.

"Any reason I shouldn't?" There was the barest note of challenge in his voice.

Because you care for me. She didn't say the words, of course, because the wish was so far from reality, and she couldn't bear it if he was to be amused at the announcement.

Because ethically you can't, since we're involved. That wasn't much better. Technically, they weren't involved—or at least, Ridge wasn't. The fact that Morea had fallen in love with him had destroyed her professional objectivity, but it didn't affect his in the least.

Which left Morea with a problem. Since he wasn't going to excuse himself from the case, she'd have to— and what would she use as a reason? She simply couldn't bear to tell the truth...

"Absolutely none," she said.

"Then why are you objecting?"

It was a reasonable question, one for which she had no good answer. "Because you said you hate divorces," she said finally. "Especially messy ones. And this one will be messy."

"Is that a threat?"

"It's a fact." Even through the thickness of the door, she could hear Trent's voice, raised in frustration, in the outer office.

Obviously Ridge heard it, too. "Perhaps you'd better see your client before he really gets out of hand."

Morea pushed herself away from the door. "He won't be my client much longer." With a flicker of relief, she recognized that Trent had presented her with the perfect excuse. "Because I won't stand for a client who behaves like that."

"You're sure that's the reason?"

"Do I need any other?"

"Of course you don't." He started toward the door, and paused. "But just in case it matters—his information is wrong. I didn't take Daisy's case." His hand was already on the doorknob by the time she could react.

"Why not?" Once started, Morea couldn't seem to stop herself, and there was no hiding the bitterness in her voice. "Because you hate messy divorces? Or because you can't stand working with me?"

He turned to look at her, and the tension in the room suddenly increased till the air seemed to sizzle.

"No, Morea. It's because I can't stand working against you."

She was confused. He'd sounded almost defiant, as if he'd intended the words as a challenge. But—

"Though even opposing you," he said more gently, "would be better than nothing at all. But since you obviously prefer that we have no contact at all—" His hand closed on the knob.

Morea flung herself at the door. Her hand brushed his sleeve, and the contact seemed to scorch her palm. Time seemed to wind down to a dead halt as she stared at him.

She never knew if he reached for her first, or if she was the one who held out her arms. But suddenly she was pressed against him, the heat of her blood seeming to weld her body to his as if they were meant to be one unit, one being...

He kissed her long and desperately, until Morea's ears were ringing and the only coherent thought she could manage was, *This is the way things are supposed to be*.

Then he set her aside. He was breathing hard; Morea

couldn't remember how to breathe at all. Her gasps wrenched at her chest like sobs.

"Sorry," Ridge said brusquely. "I didn't intend to do that. And I didn't mean to upset you again. But if you need reasons—*that's* why I turned down Daisy Paxton's case."

She watched the doorknob turn under his long fingers, and said, "Don't you dare walk out on me, Ridge!"

He paused, but he didn't let go of the knob. And he didn't speak.

The ball's in your court, Morea, she told herself. "You—" Her voice was little more than a squeak. She cleared her throat and tried again. "Does that mean you care about me?"

He muttered something she didn't quite catch. Then, sounding annoyed, he said, "No, I behave this way with every attorney I come up against. Dammit, Morea, if you must have your pound of flesh—"

"Because I think...I know...I care about you."

For the space of a dozen seconds the office was absolutely quiet. Neither of them moved. Neither of them blinked. Neither of them breathed.

The second kiss was better. It was less ferocious, less driven, more tender. It was also slower—infinitely slower—and when Ridge finally raised his head Morea was content to sink against him, with her head against his shoulder so she could listen to the rapid beating of his heart.

He nestled her close. "The last time I kissed you, in the parking garage, you were so stunned, so upset..."

"Well, I'd never been kissed quite so effectively before. And I *was* upset. You were shaking up a lot of my ideas. I didn't know what was happening to me."

"I thought I'd gone too far," he confessed huskily. "Scared you till you'd never let me close again. And the next night, at Bradley's cocktail party, you were so watchful, so wary, that I was sure of it. The instant you caught sight of me, it was like shutters closing over your face. And you were so damned eager to convince me there was no reason to quit the Madison case that I concluded you were telling me there was no chance you'd ever think of me as anything but an opponent.''

"And I," Morea said softly, "was hoping you'd admit that your reason was more than just appearances."

Ridge looked stunned. "Did I say it was?"

"I thought you did. So, when you wouldn't admit it, I concluded that you'd only been teasing again."

"Teasing?" Ridge's voice was wry. "Do you think I flirt like this with every female attorney I come across?"

"I don't know," Morea said simply. "I only know how you are with me."

"It was the only way to get your attention. As long as we had cases pending, I couldn't ask you out. And it seemed we just went from one case to the next, without a break between."

Morea ran her mind back over the last year. He was right, she realized. Ever since their first encounter in the Simmons case, they'd had something pending all the time. "You laughed when I first told you Mother's grand idea about us dating," she reminded.

"I was surprised—and a little annoyed that the idea had so obviously never occurred to you."

"Oh," she said softly. "I hadn't quite looked at it that way. I guess as long as I saw you regularly, I didn't want to ask if there was anything more going on."

"Well, I did. In fact, I tried to find a way to ask if we could change the work rules, take some time to find out if we really had something special. But even asking would have meant an end to business as usual. After I'd once admitted I found you terribly attractive, we could never go back to the relationship we had before, even if you turned me down cold. And if you did, I'd be left with nothing. I couldn't even see you in court, or in conferences.''

Morea knew how that felt. She held him just a little closer.

"So I waited, and I kept dropping hints which you never seemed to pick up,'' Ridge said softly. "And every time I saw you, I fell a little more in love.''

She was feeling a bit giddy, as if she'd suddenly found herself aboard a rocket shooting from despair to glory. "And ultimately you turned down Daisy Paxton for me,'' she teased. "What a sacrifice!''

He held her a little away from him, his eyes narrowed, and then laughed. "I want you to know it was a terrible concession. It ranks right up there with you giving up the Husband from Hell.''

"I've never liked Trent,'' Morea admitted. "I've never wanted his case. But I wouldn't have quit, either— except that I'm in love with you, and I could never again fight you.'' She frowned. "Not in court, at least.''

"Oh, that warning really relieves my mind. That's why the only sensible thing is for us to practice together, you know.''

Morea shook her head. "I'm not sure that's smart. I still don't agree with you about Daddy's case.''

"I know. If I'd pursued it—''

"It's not that. If you'd just warned me of his decision—''

"I knew that was going to blow up in my face, and there wasn't a thing I could do. Charles refused to let me bring you in. Even when I told him flat-out that you were in the thing up to your ears—''

"You told him that?''

"Not only that. He also knows how hopelessly in love with you I am, he knows that our supposed dating relationship is a farce, he knows...''

"You told him *all* that? Why?''

"I was trying, my darling, to convince him to make you a full half of his legal team, which he absolutely refused to do."

Morea considered that, and nodded. "He wanted me to be a daughter, not an attorney."

"Well, maybe he's onto something. I'm more interested in having you as my wife than my partner, though I still think—"

"Wife." She'd never realized before what a beautiful sound the word made.

"That's the deal. You don't have to join my practice—"

"I will think about it, Ridge. I just don't think I'm ready to make the decision."

"That's fair. I won't hurry you. I won't even insist that you take my name. But you have to marry me, or I'll sue you."

"For *what*?"

"I'll find a loophole somewhere."

"All right, if you're going to be difficult about it, I'll marry you."

Ridge grinned. "I'm glad you're seeing reason. I'll get right to work on the prenuptial contract."

Morea was suddenly serious. "Ridge, I really don't think—"

"You said once you wouldn't get married without one."

"I know I did, but that was before..." Her voice trailed off. It sounded so hopelessly romantic to say that there would be no need for such a thing, because their marriage couldn't fail.

"Before you fell in love?" Ridge said helpfully. "But you see, darling, that's the biggest problem. When people fall in love, all their common sense goes out the window. No—we definitely need an agreement." He pulled out his fountain pen and reached for the nearest bit of paper, a business card from the holder on her desk. "Nice card. Which reminds me, I need to get around to ordering mine."

"I'll get you some for a wedding gift. Along with a new chair."

Ridge didn't look up. "I *like* my chair."

"For the other side of your desk, in case I want to come and visit."

He smiled. "Are you certain you wouldn't rather just share mine? I thought it was fun. Here." He held out the card. "One handy-dandy prenuptial contract. Never let it be said I'm slow when it comes to important legal work."

Reluctantly, Morea turned the card over. He'd covered the back with black ink, his handwriting smaller than usual but as distinctively spiky as ever.

For better or worse, he'd written, *for richer or poorer, in sickness and in health, till death do us part.*

"Now that," Morea said, "is a contract I can live with."

"We'll take the rest as it comes," Ridge whispered, and held her close.

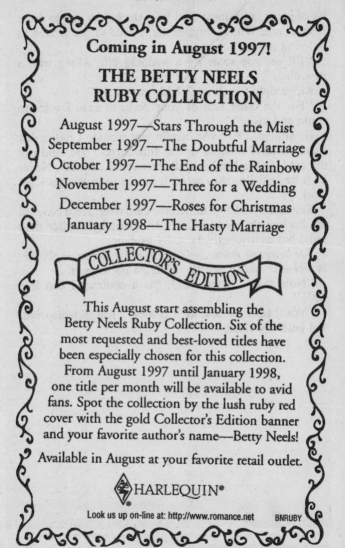

Coming in August 1997!

THE BETTY NEELS
RUBY COLLECTION

August 1997—Stars Through the Mist
September 1997—The Doubtful Marriage
October 1997—The End of the Rainbow
November 1997—Three for a Wedding
December 1997—Roses for Christmas
January 1998—The Hasty Marriage

COLLECTOR'S EDITION

This August start assembling the
Betty Neels Ruby Collection. Six of the
most requested and best-loved titles have
been especially chosen for this collection.
From August 1997 until January 1998,
one title per month will be available to avid
fans. Spot the collection by the lush ruby red
cover with the gold Collector's Edition banner
and your favorite author's name—Betty Neels!

Available in August at your favorite retail outlet.

HARLEQUIN®

HARLEQUIN WOMEN KNOW ROMANCE WHEN THEY SEE IT.

And they'll see it on **ROMANCE CLASSICS**, the new 24-hour TV channel devoted to romantic movies and original programs like the special **Harlequin® Showcase of Authors & Stories.**

The **Harlequin® Showcase of Authors & Stories** introduces you to many of your favorite romance authors in a program developed exclusively for Harlequin® readers.

Watch for the **Harlequin® Showcase of Authors & Stories** series beginning in the summer of 1997.

If you're not receiving ROMANCE CLASSICS, call your local cable operator or satellite provider and ask for it today!

Escape to the network of your dreams.

The Gentleman & THE HELL RAISER

Don't miss these captivating stories
from two acclaimed authors
of historical romance.

THE GENTLEMAN by Kristin James
THE HELL RAISER by Dorothy Glenn

Two brothers on a collision course
with destiny and love.

Find out how the dust settles October 1997
wherever Harlequin and Silhouette
books are sold.

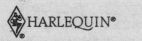

HARLEQUIN®   Silhouette®